Praise for Patricia Guiver's Pet Detective Mysteries

"*The Purloined Pooch* may be Patricia Guiver's first mystery, but it reads like the work of a seasoned pro. Her narration flows smoothly from scene to scene. Drama builds from the initial discovery of the first body to the final denouement.... Part of the charm of this delightful series debut includes how very British Dee remains despite her many years in America."

—*Mystery News*

"Humor mixed with pets of all kinds and plenty of unsavory villains leads to murder and mayhem [in *The Motley Mutts*]. This is definitely an animal lovers' delight, but anyone will get a kick out of Delilah and her motley crew. A perfect blending of pet antics, human characters, humor, and mystery."

—*Rendezvous*

"The latest addition to Patricia Guiver's 'pet detective mystery series' is as witty and entertaining as the wonderful previous works. *The Careless Coyote* includes a first-rate mystery, but the novel, filled with interesting trivia, will especially be enjoyed by Anglophiles and animal lovers."

—*Midwest Book Review*

"*The Missing Macaw* is a charming mystery with pet lore, sure to delight the animal and mystery lover. Patricia Guiver not only spins a fine tale but she presents the reader with fascinating information about pets in general and the black market for rare animals."

—*Romantic Times Magazine*

"Few books give me more pleasure than a new Delilah Doolittle.... Guiver depicts the varied locales authentically. And her gift for dialogue makes each character distinct and memorable. In fact, Pat Guiver's voice is her strong suit. ...Animal lovers are going to gobble [*The Canine Chorus*] up! Best 'brew-up' before starting it. You'll feel the need for a 'cuppa' too, before long."

—Geraldine Galantree, *Cozies, Capers & Crimes*

The Beastly Bloodline

Also by PATRICIA GUIVER

THE PET DETECTIVE SERIES

Delilah Doolittle and the Purloined Pooch
Delilah Doolittle and the Motley Mutts
Delilah Doolittle and the Careless Coyote
Delilah Doolittle and the Missing Macaw
Delilah Doolittle and the Canine Chorus

The Beastly Bloodline

A DELILAH DOOLITTLE PET DETECTIVE MYSTERY

Patricia Guiver

2003 · Palo Alto / McKinleyville, California
Perseverance Press / John Daniel & Company

This is a work of fiction. Characters, places, and events are the product of the author's imagination or are used fictitiously. Any resemblance to real people, companies, institutions, organizations, or incidents is entirely coincidental.

Printed in the United States of America

A PERSEVERANCE PRESS BOOK
Published by John Daniel & Company
A division of Daniel & Daniel, Publishers, Inc.
Post Office Box 2790
McKinleyville, California 95519
www.danielpublishing.com/perseverance

Book design by Eric Larson, Studio E Books, Santa Barbara
www.studio-e-books.com

Cover illustration: Pati Sullivan

10 9 8 7 6 5 4 3 2 1

LIBRARY OF CONGRESS CATALOGING-IN-PUBLICATION DATA
Guiver, Patricia.
The beastly bloodline : a Delilah Doolittle pet detective mystery / by Patricia Guiver.—
1st American pbk. ed.
p. cm.
ISBN 1-880284-69-3 (alk. paper)
1. Doolittle, Delilah (Fictitious character)—Fiction. 2. Women private investigators—West (U.S.)—Fiction. 3. Horses—Crimes against—Fiction. 4. British—West (U.S.)—Fiction. 5. Horsemen and horsewomen—Fiction. 6. Ranch life—Fiction. I. Title.
PS3607.U543B43 2003
813'.6—dc21
2003003907

DEDICATED TO

Redwings Horse Sanctuary

United Pegasus Foundation

Wild Horse Sanctuary

I have never cared to read about animal suffering, no matter how satisfying the eventual outcome. Certainly, I have no wish to inflict such reading upon others. Writing the Delilah Doolittle stories provides me with a welcome relief from the cruelty and ignorance I sometimes encounter in my volunteer work on behalf of animals. Even so, as I wrote this book, the plight of unwanted horses was never far from my mind.

The high-priced racehorse past its prime, the unadoptable wild mustang, the pet horse abandoned by an owner unable to afford its keep: many of these unfortunate animals end up at feedlots on their way to slaughter. It is to those horses, and the fine organisations who work to rescue and rehabilitate them, that this book is dedicated.

ACKNOWLEDGMENTS

Writing is a solitary business, nevertheless no book of mine would see the light of day if not for reassurance that I'm on the right track, and expert advice to save me from myself.

Among those I wish to thank for their support and generous input are my fellow authors in the Fictionaires writers' group, and in particular, Patricia McFall for her unfailing encouragement and faith in me.

Thanks are also due to Dr. Julie Ann Ryan Johnson, veterinarian and expert horsewoman, for reviewing the manuscript. Any errors remaining within these pages are mine alone.

Cast of Characters

People

Delilah Doolittle, *pet detective*
Evie Cavendish, *her best friend*
Tiptoe Tony Tipton, *Cockney senior surfer and petty thief, retired (he claims)*
Detective Jack Mallory, *Surf City P.D. Homicide Division*
Sergeant William Offley, *Surf City P.D.*
Hilda Dorsett-Bragg, *horse breeder; distant cousin to Evie*
Robert Dorsett-Bragg, *her son*
Fiona Dorsett-Bragg, *her daughter, and Evie's godchild*
Joseph Dorsett, *deceased, Hilda's father*
Daniel Bragg, *deceased, Hilda's husband*
Lucy Dorsett-Bragg, *Robert's wife, niece of*
Doris Carpenter, *wife of*
Hank Carpenter, *horse farm manager, father of*
Buck Carpenter, *dude ranch manager*
Donald (Scottie) MacDonald, *caretaker of mission church*
Charles Bragg, *Hilda's brother-in-law*
Austin Tully, DVM, *horse vet*
Seymour Hicks, *accountant*
Anna Banning, *local sheriff*
Dr. George Kendall, his wife Marsha, and two sons, *guests*
Rusty, *a wrangler*
Curly, *chuckwagon driver*

Animals

Watson, *Delilah's Doberman sidekick, confidante, and protector*
Trixie, *Tony's Jack Russell terrier*
Chamois, *Evie's Maltese terrier*
Hobo, *a three-legged feral cat*
Dolly, *Delilah's cockatiel*
The Duke of Paddington, *champion stud horse*
The Duchess of Bayswater, *Fiona's horse*
Nifty, *Hilda's Yorkshire terrier*
Assorted mutts, *owned by Scottie*

The Beastly Bloodline

CHAPTER I

Death of a Duke

The morning I learned the shocking news about the Duke of Paddington, Watson and Trixie were having a bark-up in the back garden and I could barely hear the caller on the other end of the line. It was unusually warm for April and I had opened the kitchen window to enjoy the breeze wafting up from the Pacific Ocean a half block from my house.

"Watson! Trixie! Quiet!" I shouted from the window.

Watson, my red Dobie, obeyed immediately, but Trixie, the Jack Russell, continued to bark at an unseen foe. Finally, the object of her wrath, Hobo, the half-wild ginger tom tripod who condescends to lodge in my garden, emerged from the oleander bushes, stretched lazily, then fixed the terrier with a rebuking stare. That not having the desired silencing effect, he fetched the dog a well-placed swat across the nose.

I closed the window, effectively muffling the sound of Trixie's yelping retreat in the direction of the doggie door.

"I'm sorry," I said to the caller. "I must have misunderstood. Did you say someone's been killed? Surely you must call the police?"

"No, not someone," the woman's voice exclaimed impatiently. "A horse. One of my prize stallions, the Duke of Paddington." She sounded older, cultured—moneyed, certainly, as she would need to be to support a stable of equine aristocrats. The monthly farrier's bill alone would no doubt be sufficient to keep me in groceries. "The police aren't interested," she was saying. "They told me to call animal control." There was a sigh of evident frustration. "Animal control said to call the police."

It was a familiar runaround. There are plenty of animal protection laws on the books but they aren't a priority with police kept busy enough with people crimes. And animal control doesn't always have the personnel or the budget to follow up on what too often turns out to be an unfounded accusation.

"And who suggested you call me?" I inquired.

"A mutual friend, Evelyn Cavendish."

"I see." Leave it to Evie to offer my services without first consulting me.

"She speaks very highly of your abilities," the woman continued, "and since our local sheriff insists that it was just an unfortunate accident, you really are my last resort."

Now it was my turn to sigh. No-one likes to be thought of as a last resort, carrying with it as it does the implication that all other possible, and no doubt superior, options have proved fruitless. It didn't say much for my chances of success, either.

I recalled Evie had said something recently about going to spend a few days at a dude ranch owned by a distant relative, Hilda Dorsett-Bragg, matriarch of a historic stud farm operation near the Cleveland National Forest in southern California. She'd mentioned her concern about Hilda's health and what she described as "peculiar goings-on" in the family. I was inclined to believe her visit had more to do with her declared intention of putting a stop to what she considered to be an undesirable match between her god-daughter, Fiona, and a local cowboy. Whatever it was, Evie had obviously lost no time in attempting to rope me into the proceedings.

Well, I wasn't going to fall for it this time. "Is Evie there?" I said.

"Yes, she is. Hold on, she wants to speak to you."

"Dee, you absolutely must come." Evie's cut-glass English accent pierced the telephone line. "Poor Hilda is *très distraite.* It's vile what's happened to that horse of hers. I shall be quite put out if you say no."

"But I know nothing about horses," I protested.

Cats and dogs, and the occasional parrot or tortoise, or rather their owners, were my usual clients. And though the pet detecting game was rather slow at the moment, I expected it to pick up any time, and I didn't want to be out of town when the calls started to come in. Summer was just around the corner. It was a time when vacationing pet-owners could be relied upon to leave their animals in the dubious care of neighbour children; when school holidays guaranteed an abundance of open gates and doors to lure unwary pets to venture abroad. Then came the July Fourth holiday weekend, when fireworks panicked hitherto sane Golden Labs and sedate Spaniels into hurling themselves through plate glass windows and bolting for the hills.

"Of course you know about horses," snapped my best friend. "You always won the blue ribbons at school gymkhanas. Remember that Shetland pony we shared? What was its name?"

"Rocky," I reminded her. It was years since I'd thought of the docile little chestnut with the long mane and tail.

"That's right. Your memory's better than mine."

"Mm," I agreed. "I also recall that my share of the stable duties was invariably larger than yours. You always managed to have a migraine or something when it came to mucking out the stalls."

"You're making that up," she accused me, only half in fun. "You were certainly the better horsewoman, so why shouldn't you do most of the chores?"

I didn't want to argue. Evie invariably had the last word, as I had learned to my cost over the years, and perhaps in this case she was right. But that had been in England many years ago. I knew nothing of the American riding culture except what I'd learned from the cinema. Visions of John Wayne and "saddlin' 'em up and movin' 'em out" came to mind. And this case was more sinister than any film. This was real life, and I was being called upon to investigate a case of suspected equine murder.

Evie broke into my thoughts. "Don't be tiresome, sweetie. Anyone would think I was asking you to ride in the Grand National." Her exasperation came through loud and clear. "Just think of it like any other animal case. You're forever carting off to God-knows-where in search of lost Pekes and Poodles. What's the difference? After all the cases you've dragged me into. How often do I ask you to do anything for me?"

Quite frequently, as a matter of fact.

Trixie had gained access to the kitchen through the doggie door and was now rolling on her back at my feet, her confrontation with the ginger tom apparently forgotten. I idly stroked her tummy with my bare foot. Her warm tongue tickled my toes, and I stifled a giggle. Here was my excuse.

"Sorry luv," I said to Evie. "Can't oblige. I'm dog-sitting."

"Dog-sitting! Oh, for heaven's sake. Don't tell me you're that strapped for cash?"

Evie could be brutally blunt at times, though as she was fond of pointing out, all she wanted was the best for me, and how I could do so much better for myself if only I'd allow her to run my life and find me what she would consider a real job, or better yet, "a rich RNM" (Really Nice Man).

This time I gave her no chance to start on such a rant, hastily interrupting with, "No. I'm helping out a friend. It's Trixie."

"Trixie?"

"Tony's Jack Russell."

"Oh, right. Where is the dear boy?" The dear boy, as she called him, was all of seventy years old. It was her term of endearment for any male who won her approval.

"He's in Australia," I answered.

"What in the world's he doing there?"

Good, I'd got her off the subject of my shortcomings. "Visiting relatives and lying low after that dust-up in Las Vegas last year," I said.

Fellow Brit Tony Tipton, or Tiptoe Tony as he was known to those more familiar with his criminal past, had come perilously close to being a prime suspect in my late husband's murder, having been one of the last people to see him alive when he'd disappeared several years earlier. Once poor Roger's ghost had finally been laid to to rest, Tony, a champion senior surfer, had headed Down Under in search of the perfect wave.

"When's he due back?"

"Not for another few days."

"Just bring both dogs with you, then. Hold on a sec." She must have put her hand over the phone. I could hear a muffled conversation on the other end. After a moment or two she was back on the line. "All taken care of. Hilda says doggies no prob. They're all over the place here. She won't notice two more. Chamois is here." Chamois was Evie's tiny Maltese.

I flipped over the mail idly as she chatted, wondering if they really planned to take stern measures with my electricity.

"Oh, all right. I'll go," I said.

"Super. Oh, and be a sweetie and bring along some of those divine dog biscuits you make. Chamois thinks they're to die for."

Of course he does.

"It shouldn't take you more than two hours to get here from Surf City, even in that clapped-out excuse of a car you drive," she continued. (She referred to my admittedly ancient Ford station wagon.) "Here's Hilda with directions."

That's the way Evie is. She'll let nothing stand in the way of what she wants, and if she can convince herself that it's all for the benefit of somebody else, so much the better. Everything's so simple for her. Born into privilege, married into wealth, she has never been able to understand the obligations and responsibilities others not similarly blessed have to deal with.

Through the window I could see Watson dozing in the shade of the pepper tree, from a lower branch of which hung a hummingbird feeder. A few feet away Hobo sat as if mesmerised by the darting winged jewels.

Evie had adroitly solved the dog problem. But what about Hobo? Feral he might be, but he had come to expect, if not depend on, daily dinner on my porch, and I didn't want to disappoint him. Then there was Dolly, my cockatiel. I couldn't just walk out the front door and forget about her. I sighed. I had too many dependents to just take off whenever I felt like it. I hoped that Ariel, my neighbour, would be able to cover for me.

Hilda Dorsett-Bragg came back on the line: "I can't tell you how much I appreciate this," she said in a tone that left me in no doubt of her sincerity. "We must find out who did this terrible thing. I'm afraid my other horses may be in danger, too."

I took my pad and pen from the shelf under the telephone and prepared to write down the directions. "Try not to worry," I said. "It'll probably turn out to have been an accident. If it wasn't, let's get all the facts and then we'll go to the police." I sounded capable and professional, but to tell the truth I felt I was venturing into uncharted territory.

"How did..." I put it as delicately as I could. "Er, what was the cause of death?"

"The autopsy indicated that it was poison."

Oh dear. That sounded premeditated. "Do you have any suspicions about who might have done such a thing? And why?"

"I can't say for sure. But a neighbour, a rival horse breeder, has made threats against me in the past."

This was interesting. "Oh. Who is that?"

There was a slight hesitation, then she said, "Charles Bragg."

"Any relation?"

"Brother-in-law." I could sense the distaste in her voice.

And what motive would he have, I wondered.

Dolly twittered in her cage, as if trying to join in the conversation, reminding me that I'd want to bring back a gift for Ariel, a thank-you for pet-sitting. That got me thinking about expenses.

I quoted my rate. "That's plus expenses, of course." Already there was mileage, and who knew whether my old banger would be able to handle those mountain roads without overheating.

Again she hesitated. "I see. You know you'll be staying at the ranch as my guest, so you won't have to pay for food or lodging."

Logical though that was, I nevertheless thought I detected a hint of parsimony in the statement. Was Evie right that the redoubtable Dorsett Farms was in financial difficulties? And had Hilda imagined that, like Evie, I was the possessor of a private income, and had taken up pet detecting as a sort of whimsical pastime? It probably hadn't occurred to Evie to be more explicit.

"I hope I'll be able to help you," I said. "But, of course, there's no guarantee of success. In either case I'd still expect my regular rate, plus out-of-pocket expenses."

"I understand. It's agreed, then. You'll be here by early afternoon tomorrow?" I murmured my assent, and was about to hang up when she added, "Oh. There's one other thing. I must insist that no-one other than ourselves, and Evelyn, of course, know the true reason for your visit. You will be introduced simply as Evelyn's friend. Is that understood?"

Why the secrecy? What was there to hide? Remaining incognito would make my job twice as difficult.

I didn't answer her demand, merely saying, "I'll see you tomorrow."

CHAPTER 2

The Mission

Dolly paused in her peck around the kitchen counter to greet her reflection in the chrome tea-kettle. Then hopping over to her morning spoonful of tea, she scooped the warm, sweet liquid into her beak, tilting her head back to let it run down her throat.

She would miss her daily ritual. "Can't be helped," I told her. "Mummy's got to go and bring home the bacon."

If her repertoire had extended beyond the first two bars of "Hello, Dolly" and a repetitious "Wake up, Birdie," the cockatiel might have chirped that being a pet detective was a rather odd way in which to earn the bacon, or in her case, the bird seed.

I would have had to agree. You won't find many of us in the Yellow Pages. Be that as it may, tracing missing pets is an occupation which, once having stumbled into, I've discovered I'm rather good at. And though being my own boss means the tangible fringes are non-existent—no paid vacation, health insurance, or pension—the intangibles are priceless: I'm out in the fresh air, and best of all, I get to take my dear Watson with me. Not to mention meeting some wonderful animals in the course of my work. Dolly herself had come my way during my search for a missing macaw.

While in the best of all possible worlds I'd prefer that every pet wear a tag and be kept safely at home, it's to the carelessness of a significant portion of the pet-owning public that I owe my livelihood.

Certainly pet detecting is not a career from which I'm likely to earn more than a modest living. But the overheads are few. Telephone, advertising, and mileage constitute the bulk of my expenses. The job doesn't require much of a wardrobe, nor does it call for anything posh in the way of transportation. My passengers are most likely to be muddy-pawed dogs or clawing cats. My beat-up station wagon is quite adequate to my needs, despite minor mechanical malfunctions like the window crank which rattles loose against the door and only works when it's in the mood.

"As long as it gets us there. That's all that counts," I said to Watson, waiting patiently on the sidewalk while I rearranged stuff in the back of the wagon to make room for my overnight bags and other necessities of the trip. The tools of my trade—cat trap; pet carrier; scarred leather gloves, veterans of disputes with cantankerous cats and peevish parrots; towels and blankets; a catchpole, a long stick with a noose-like arrangement at one end; jerky treats and tins of sardines to lure the reluctant runaway—were shoved to one side. None of it would be any use in solving the mystery of the dead horse. But I was planning to be away for several days, and one never knew what other animal emergencies might arise.

Trixie bounded in as soon as I lowered the tailgate. No doubt she thought she was going home to Tony.

"Sorry, ducks," I said to the little white, black, and tan bundle of mischief. "Your dad's not back yet. You're going to have to come and meet the gees-gees with me and Watson."

It had occurred to me more than once since my conversation with Evie that taking an energetic Jack Russell to a stud farm might not have been the wisest of decisions. She must have forgotten how much of a handful Trixie can be. Too late now.

But to be on the safe side, I'd left a message on Tony's machine to the effect that if I wasn't home by the time he returned, he was to come to Dorsett Farms to collect his dog as soon as possible.

Blissfully ignorant of the anxiety she was causing me, Trixie sniffed at the dog biscuit tin, then turned a hopeful look in my direction. "Not for you, ducks," I started to say, then relented. Why make cookies for Chamois, who, much as I loved the little Maltese, lacked for absolutely nothing, then deny my own, well, not exactly flesh and blood, but certainly members of my extended family.

Trixie must have read my mind. She sat up on the tailgate and begged. I placed a bone-shaped biscuit on her nose, as I had often seen Tony do. "Here you are then." With a quick toss of her head she flipped the treat into her mouth. "Good girl," I said.

Watson nudged the back of my knee. "All right, all right. You know I'd never leave you out." I gave her two of the biscuits. "Double for you because you're bigger."

Ariel had readily agreed to keep a friendly eye on Dolly and Hobo. In return, I'd promised to be back in time to take care of Lulu, her Peke, while she was on vacation. So, after returning for the umpteenth time to check that the doggie door was locked to prevent Hobo from getting in to satisfy his curiosity as to the source of the "Hello, Dolly" melody, we were on our way.

After a few miles south on Interstate 5, I turned inland towards the Santa Ana Mountains and was soon driving through a rural area dotted with orange and avocado groves on low-lying hills, with roadside hedges entwined with flowering vines replacing the vivid reds and purples of coastal ice plant and bougainvillea.

As I drove, I tried to recall what else Evie had told me over the years about Hilda Dorsett-Bragg. Hilda was a distant cousin, she'd said, whose family had emigrated to America two generations earlier. The horse farm had been established by Hilda's grandfather with stock brought over from England. The dude ranch had been added more recently when an additional source of income had become necessary. Evie rattles on so, I'm afraid I don't always give her my full attention, but I did remember something about Hilda being upset because her son had married "beneath" him. Was that what she'd meant by "peculiar goings-on?"

The road climbed on past wildlife habitat and a wilderness park, home to mountain lions and red-tailed hawks. Flowering shrubs gave way to oaks, sycamores, and pines, their deep green branches tipped with spring's tender new needles of palest green.

The air was cooler at this elevation, and I was glad I'd worn a light sweater with my T-shirt and jeans.

The sun was still quite high, slanting rays through the young foliage and dappling the road surface with sunlight and shadow when we began a slow descent into a lush green valley.

A sign for the Santa Ana Bird Sanctuary jogged my memory to the belated realisation that I hadn't let Jack know I was leaving town. Jack being Detective Jack Mallory, the "token" man in my life, as Evie calls him, meaning someone who'd do until a chap she considers to be more suitable comes along.

Jack and I hadn't been on the best of terms lately. We'd had the silliest disagreement. Both of us bird lovers, we'd gone to the Surf City wetlands to watch for the visiting waterfowl who stop by during the spring migration. Unexpectedly, we'd found ourselves at odds over the identity of a bird not usually seen this far north. Was it a masked or a blue-footed booby? I had been ready to agree that it was one or the other, and that to see either was exciting, and now let's go home. My feet were freezing and thoughts of a nice cup of tea were fast over-riding the booby debate. But Mallory, who lectured on birds at the local college, was bent on making a definitive identification to add to his life list. He is a hard-core birder—no mountain too high, no canyon too deep, et cetera. I, on the other hand, relish being outdoors, enjoying the birds relatively easy to spot, but content to know on good authority when something significant is on the wing. That's why my life list remains a scant couple of pages, while Jack's is well on the way to completion.

Exasperated, he urged me to use his powerful scope to verify his find. But try as I might, I couldn't make the distinction. "I'm sorry. It's hard to tell from here. The reeds are in the way, but I think it's the blue-footed. Either that, or its feet are cold from being in the water all this time. I know mine are."

But Jack's normally ready sense of humour seemed to have temporarily deserted him. With a sigh of annoyance he picked up the scope and stalked off to look for a better vantage point.

I called after him. "I think it's bloody marvellous, whichever it is. You should be satisfied with that. Let's go."

But the lure of the booby was too strong. He stayed, and I walked home, taking the short cut along the path that led to my back garden. That was a week ago, and we hadn't spoken since.

A tricky bend in the road brought my attention back to the present. Watson, sitting beside me on the slick leather seat, shifted her weight as we rounded the corner. "When you're a recognised authority on birds I suppose it's rather galling to be told you can't distinguish between a masked and a blue-footed booby," I said to her. "But why does he have to be so damned earnest about it?"

Watson opened and closed one soulful brown eye, in a gesture I've come to recognise as her way of expressing doubt.

"You're right, of course. I should have apologised," I said. Watson and I often commune in this manner when we're on the road. I invariably find the insights that she's able to convey through the slightest body language or facial expression to be helpful. "It was obviously important to him, and I shouldn't have treated it so casually. I'll call him when we get there."

"Hasn't he proposed yet?" Evie had asked just the other day. "I thought after Las Vegas you two had become a lot closer."

It was true the relationship had deepened since we worked together on the Canine Chorus case, but there had been no suggestion of anything permanent.

"No, and not likely to," I'd responded. "We're both too set in our ways to make any abrupt changes." But recalling her words prompted me to wonder what my response would be if Mallory should propose.

"Not to worry, Watson, old girl. For the time being we'll keep our options open. I'm not rushing into anything. Look where romantic impulse got us the last time."

My last venture into matrimony had been with the late, unlamented Roger, who had turned out to be a cad of the first order. His larcenous ways had eventually landed him in more trouble than he could handle and he'd ended up dead in the Mojave Desert, murdered in a real estate scam gone sour.

Jack Mallory was cut from a completely different bolt of cloth. Although we'd had our differences in the early days of our acquaintance, and still did on occasion, witness the recent booby incident, I had come to respect and appreciate the kind and decent man under the stern policeman's exterior.

We came to a fork in the road where a grassy mound held numerous Forest Service warnings of fire hazards. It had been an unusually dry winter, and the forests were at high risk in the approaching hot season. Another sign caught my eye. HORSE SHOW CLASSIC. SPONSORED BY DORSETT FARMS. "We're getting close, ladies," I told my canine companions.

Following Hilda's directions I turned off the highway onto a two-lane road, passing stables, white-fenced exercise pens, and well-kept farms. Old oak trees canopied across the road. Two young girls on horseback waved as I passed. I felt time slowing down. Maybe I was going to enjoy my assignment after all.

Another turn and the road narrowed still more. With the slowing down and the turns, Watson and Trixie had become restless, sensing we'd be stopping soon. "I'd better let you out for a tinkle somewhere along here," I told them. "Once we get to the ranch there's no knowing when we'll have another opportunity."

Up ahead in a quiet, secluded setting, was an old mission church, early California style, with white adobe walls and red tile roof, a bell tower to one side. A low moss-covered stone wall surrounded a graveyard filled with weathered markers. This would be the Santa Ana Mission that Hilda had told me to watch for. A nearby clearing offered a convenient parking spot.

I pulled over. "This will do," I said. But as I opened the car door my sweater sleeve caught on the loose window crank, and the impatient Watson and Trixie were out before I had a chance to snap on their leashes.

As I fiddled to extricate the yarn I heard a low growl and a disturbance behind me. Turning, I saw Watson and Trixie, their backs against the wall, cornered by several large brown dogs of uncertain breed and temperament. They were quite obviously spoiling for a fight.

CHAPTER 3

The Horseman

The dogs stood silent and menacing, waiting for their leader, a rangy, lean and hungry-looking creature, to make a move. My first thought was that they were one of those marauding packs that band together for food and protection after being abandoned in the back country.

They were between me and Watson and Trixie who, having given up on their futile attempts to escape over the wall, looked at me for guidance in the face of this display of uncalled-for incivility. Trixie cowered behind Watson, whose stance declared that, though she'd much rather not, she would fight to the death if need be.

One false move was all it would take to set that in motion. Keeping one wary eye on the pack, I slowly backed up to the open car door, reached in, and groped for the catchpole. Not that I had any intention of snaring one of the offending animals. I just feel braver with some kind of weapon in my hands.

My heart in my mouth, I edged forward, placing myself between the pack and my dogs. Then stretching up to my full five feet one, I shouted, "I say! Get out of here! Bad dogs! Go home!" The leader turned on me with a nasty snarl, but backed off when he saw the catchpole and started to bark. His mates soon joined in.

I was contemplating my next move when I became aware of an elderly man hurrying toward us waving a large stick. He wore denim overalls over a plaid shirt, a red tam-o'-shanter pulled down over white hair. His mouth was opening and closing, but I couldn't hear a word over the barking. Finally, in a rare moment when the dogs all paused for breath at the same time, I heard him say, "Ian, Jock, Mack. Get on home, ye mangy beasties." The brogue was Scottish, but the stick he carried was Irish, a shillelagh, if memory served.

The barking abated to low growls.

"Are these your animals?" I demanded.

"Och aye, lassie, they are," he replied. "Did ye ever see a finer flock?"

He stood admiring his fine flock, oblivious of the threat they were to me and my dogs, and made no further effort to call them off.

"Please do something," I yelled to him as loudly as I dared. "They have my dogs cornered." But he shrugged his shoulders helplessly, and shuffled off, glancing back toward the mission every few steps as if to assure himself that I was still there.

The sound of horse's hooves on the roadway broke the stand-off. Pulling my gaze from the pack I watched the approach of a man astride a white horse. It took only a second or two for him to assess the situation, then, spurring the horse forward into the pack, he sent them scattering after the old man.

Watson and Trixie wasted no time in dashing back to the safety of the car. I closed the door after them.

The horseman rode over to the car, coming so close I could feel the horse's warm breath on my face. He pushed his cowboy hat back from a tanned forehead, revealing grey, close-cropped hair. Late fifties, I guessed, extremely fit.

"Are you okay?" His voice was strong, amused.

"Thanks," I said, tossing the catchpole through the open car window. "You came along just in time. Who is that person?"

"Old Scottie? He's caretaker for the mission. He lives over there." He pointed to a small, unprepossessing cottage a few yards further down the road, barely visible behind overgrown bushes and weeds. "The dogs are harmless," the stranger finished with a smile.

"Not to me and my dogs, they're not," I said with a regrettable sharpness clearly not intended for my white knight, my only excuse being I was quite shaken by the experience. "Somebody should speak to him about keeping his animals under control."

"There's usually not much traffic along this road," he said. "Where're you headed?"

I was about to say, "Dorsett Farms," when I realised that he might be a neighbour of Hilda Dorsett-Bragg, and I was supposed to be here incognito. "The Lazy D Guest Ranch," I said. "Is this the right road?"

I thought I detected a flicker of displeasure cross his face. If so, he hid it quickly, and said, "The dude ranch? Keep going and you'll see the sign on your left. You can't miss it."

With a tip of his hat, he reined the horse around and was gone before I had a chance to thank him properly.

"What an interesting man," I said to Watson. "I wonder what Evie would make of him. She'd never have let him get away before she'd found out his marital status, social connections, and finances."

But the Dobie ignored me. She was busy licking a jagged scratch on her foreleg. She must have been hurt in her scramble to escape the mangy beasties. "Oh, nasty," I said. "Never mind. I'll take care of it as soon as we're settled in."

I drove on another half a mile or so, passing white fences and meadows where horses grazed or dozed under shady oaks. Before long we came to a free-standing wooden sign with black and gold letters painted on white. LAZY D GUEST RANCH, OWNED AND OPERATED BY DORSETT FARMS, HOME OF CHAMPIONS SINCE 1905. A wide driveway led to a one-storey building, with white stucco walls and a red tile roof. To the right lay a well-manicured lawn, beyond that a swimming pool where several people sat around on lounge chairs.

To the left of the driveway was a covered round pen where a teenage boy sat on the fence watching a young woman in jeans, shirt, and hard hat put a horse through its paces on a lunge line.

I parked the car and was immediately welcomed by two large and amiable Golden Retrievers. Watson and Trixie were eager to get out and exchange sniffed greetings, but I had learned my lesson. They could wait in the car until I had registered and received directions to the cabin I was to share with Evie.

Before entering the lobby I checked the map by the entrance. It showed two distinct properties—the guest ranch with its cabins, stables, bunkhouse, swimming pool, and tennis courts, and further to the north, Dorsett House, which would be the large English-style manor house I could see from where I stood. Beyond the house was a section marked DORSETT STABLES, with the words NO ADMITTANCE EXCEPT BY APPOINTMENT written on the map in red marker pen. Obviously the family made quite a distinction between the family spread and the dude ranch. Outlying boundaries indicated pastures and fenced acreage, bordered on two sides by national forest.

I was about to follow the Goldens into the lobby when a voice called, "Yoo-hoo, Delilah."

I turned to see a middle-aged blond woman tripping towards me from the direction of the swimming pool. She wore a large floppy hat, high heels, and a short flowered wrap. One hand flourished a long cigarette holder, the other clutched a small white dog.

CHAPTER 4

The Best Friend

"Delilah! Here you are at last!" Evie's cultured tones fluted across the lawn in the still afternoon air. "I've been watching for you this past hour. Did you get lost? Where have you been?" All uttered without pausing long enough for me to respond. If she'd given me half a chance I'm sure she'd have been most intrigued to hear about the encounter with the pack of dogs and the mysterious horseman.

Nevertheless it was with genuine pleasure that I hugged her and Chamois, her little Maltese. It had been a month or so since we'd seen each other, and much as she could try one's patience, at heart she was a good, loyal friend.

"Never mind about checking in," she said, as I was about to enter the lobby. "You can do that later. Let me get in and I'll show you the way."

I readily agreed. I was anxious to get settled and desperate for a cup of tea. The run-in with the dogs had unnerved me more than I had been willing to admit to the handsome stranger.

Evie removed her cigarette from its holder and stubbed it out with a delicate shoe tip on the gravel driveway. "Silly rule," she said in a wry tone as she and Chamois settled into the passenger seat. "Smokers are exiled to the pool area."

She looked with distaste at my car's torn upholstery, legacy of a break-in during our Las Vegas adventure. "Why are you still driving this decrepit vehicle? No wonder it took you so long to get here. It's a miracle you made it at all. Howard says you ought to…" Mercifully I was spared her husband's directive, issued, I'm sure, at her prompting. Catching sight of the young woman in the round pen, she rolled down the window and called, "Yoo-hoo, Fiona. Delilah's here. See you at dinner, sweetie."

The girl waved back as Evie continued, "That's Fiona, my godchild. I told you all about her. Just back from university in England. Beautiful child, but headstrong, like her mother. I'm afraid coming home was not entirely a good idea. She's taken a fancy to one of the ranch hands. Not at all suitable." She sighed. I hate to admit it, but Evie is a bit of a snob, and considers it her bounden duty to ensure that all her friends and relations keep their feet firmly on the upward rungs of the social ladder.

"Don't do that, sweetie," she chided Trixie, who was climbing on the back of her seat trying to sniff at Chamois. Then to me, "I don't know why you must cart along a menagerie every time you go anywhere. Surely someone else could have minded Tony's dog."

"He entrusted her to my care. Besides, I'm not about to palm her off on some unsuspecting neighbour; she's too much of a handful. And she'd have been miserable boarded at the vet's." I didn't add that I'd have been lucky to get the boarding fee reimbursed, Tony not being one to put his hand in his pocket too readily.

Driving slowly, we made our way on a dirt road through a scattering of pine trees, with cabins interspersed at random.

"Pull in here," Evie directed, as we approached a cabin painted white with green trim.

Our feet scrunched on the pine needle carpet, sending up a pleasantly fresh scent.

"We'll be roughing it, I'm afraid," she said.

Roughing it was not the way I would have described our accommodation. The cabin was only slightly smaller than my bungalow in Surf City. To one side of the sitting room two doors opened onto bedrooms. Beyond the sitting room was a kitchenette.

"Only one bathroom," said Evie. "I hope that won't be a problem?"

"Not for me," I said. Though I guessed it might well be for her, given the hours she took with her make-up and hair. I'd do my best to stay out of her way.

"This is heavenly," I said, sinking into a butter-soft leather arm chair, ready for a rest. A nudge from Watson reminded me that the dogs needed to be fed and watered. I dragged myself to my feet and made for the kitchen. With Watson and Trixie impatiently dancing around my feet, I put down a water bowl and a dish of kibble for each of them. Chamois viewed this display of high spirits with alarm and retreated to safety behind the couch.

Evie took a bottle of Beefeater's from the sideboard. "What would you like to drink? G and T?"

Gin and tonic could wait until later. "Tea for me. I'm gasping."

"The makings are in the kitchen. Help yourself." Presumably she considered her hostess duties had been discharged.

"No thanks. I've brought my own." From one of my two overnight bags I removed a Brown Betty teapot, china cup and saucer, a packet of Red Rose tea-bags, and some shortbread biscuits.

Evie put down the Beefeater's. "Oh, you brought the good stuff. In that case I'll join you. But if you drag out one of your Great-aunt Nell's knitted tea-cosies, I swear I'll make make you wear it," she declared.

"Hey, don't laugh. It might come in handy if the nights get chilly."

A few minutes later, we took our tea outside to the porch.

"It's so peaceful here," I said, savouring the tall pines reaching into the clear blue sky, the crisp mountain air, the only sounds the screeching blue jays and chattering squirrels. "Where is everybody?"

"Most of them are out on a day's ride. They'll be back in time for dinner. You'll meet them all this evening, along with the family, ranch hands, and staff. A sort of debriefing when everyone shares the day's experiences. Of course, since the horse died there's been little talk of anything else. Hilda's terribly cut up."

I had to admit that I'd been avoiding thinking about the real reason for my visit, so absorbed was I with my new surroundings and the encounter at the mission.

"How's she taking it?"

"Well, she's over the shock, but absolutely devastated. That horse was the last of the line her grandfather brought over from England back in nineteen-aught-something."

I helped myself to another shortbread finger, accidentally dropping a piece to the floor. Trixie and Watson scrambled in their zeal to help tidy up. From Evie's lap Chamois gazed in wide-eyed wonder at their temerity.

I offered Evie the packet of shortbread. "No more for me, sweetie. Dinner's at seven. Provincially early, I know, but everyone's supposed to be up at dawn's crack. Hilda insists on us all taking meals together at the big house. Drearily Victorian it is, too. But there's not a crumb to be had anywhere else, so it's either that or go without. It's her way of keeping tabs on us all. Most of the guests seem to love it. A throwback to the old days, I suppose."

"She sounds a bit of a tartar," I said.

"Absolutely. She runs the place with the proverbial iron fist in velvet glove. Even though she had to give up the physical management after her stroke a couple of years ago, there's no question about who's boss. She was so put out when her son, Robert, married without her permission, she threatened to disinherit him."

"And did she?"

"Not sure if she actually went through with it. I doubt it. She absolutely dotes on the boy. But he's a major disappointment all around. Refuses to take over the reins here. That's why she had to hire someone. And he's not the teeniest bit interested in the horses. Not like Fiona."

"Oh yes. We saw her when I arrived."

"Her daughter, my godchild. That's why I'm here. She'll be

twenty-one in a few days, and she's riding in a horse show the same day as well. Wild horses couldn't keep me away." She put a hand to her cheek. "Talking of wild horses, I've been meaning to tell you, there's a horse refuge nearby. I thought you'd want to know, being such a nature lover."

That was interesting. I hoped I'd have a chance to check it out while I was in the area.

Evie's delicate brow furrowed. "One can't help worrying about her. Fiona, I mean. Brilliant child. She could do anything she set her mind to. Regretfully, right now, it seems to be set on pursuing a relationship with this ranch hand, Buck. He runs the dude ranch side of the business. His father's Hank Carpenter, the farm manager. Well, if he thinks he's going to marry Fiona and get his hands on the family business, he's got another think coming. He's got me to deal with. That's another reason I'm here. Hilda hopes I'll be able to influence her." Her eyes hardened.

I didn't like that look. "Maybe it's just a spring fling," I consoled her. "She's probably letting off steam after working hard at school. She'll get over it."

I marvelled that the whole time we'd been chatting Evie hadn't lit a cigarette, and said so.

"Poolside only," she reminded me, thrusting her lower lip forward in a pout. "Silly rule. Not even allowed in the cabin. Absurd, isn't it? The young Buck's fanatic about it. But not to worry. I've found a secret spot, quite nearby. No-one ever goes there, and the heavenly honeysuckle masks the smoke."

I watched Watson gently worrying at a pine cone. Trixie, having been warned off with a quiet growl, was sniffing the base of a nearby pine, while a pair of blue jays scolded her from above.

The birds reminded me that I needed to call Jack. "Where's the phone?" I said. "I have to make a call."

"Another silly rule. No phones in the cabins. I told you we'd be roughing it," she said with a touch of annoyance. "We have to use the pay phone in the lobby. My cell phone's useless way out here."

Well, at least that would be a refreshing change. My telephone rang constantly at home. My ad in the local lost-and-found classifieds attracted a wide variety of animal-related calls, as if a talent for locating lost pets implied a fount of knowledge on every possible aspect of animal care and behaviour. I was happy to help when I could, and the contacts were sometimes good for business.

I returned to the subject at hand. "Who did Robert marry, that Hilda should disapprove so strongly?"

"A girl named Lucy. She's a step-relative, niece or some such of the farm manager's wife. That's the problem. Hilda thinks that they encouraged her to set her cap at Robert. Then if their son Buck could land Fiona they'd be in a fair way to controlling the entire business. That's the reason Hilda keeps Robert tied so close to her purse strings."

It all sounded a bit paranoid to me, and I wondered what bearing, if any, this tale of smotherly love might have on the mystery of the dead horse.

"Is that what you think?" I asked.

"Good heavens, I hardly know them. But I feel for Hilda. She sees it as a total betrayal." Evie sipped her tea thoughtfully. "I wouldn't say it to her face, of course, but Robert has done exactly the same as she did."

"What's that?"

"Married against her parents' wishes. And look where that led," she declared emphatically.

"Where, exactly?"

"Hilda defied the family and eloped with a neighbouring ne'er-do-well, Daniel Bragg. Bit of a bounder by all accounts. Turned out to be brutal with it." As if anticipating my question, she said hurriedly, "I never met him, a bit before my time, of course. All Hilda's father could do was insist that the children would be named Dorsett-Bragg. That started the rift between the two families that got worse when Daniel died. Terrible thing. A shooting accident."

"Who shot him?"

"Joseph Dorsett. Hilda's father. I don't know the details. Hilda's always been closed-mouthed about it. It's all rather fraught. They said the old man's eyesight was failing and he should never have been allowed to handle a gun. But I remember my father telling me that Joe Dorsett was an expert marksman till the day he died. Ancient history now, of course. But the Braggs carry the grudge to this day."

I began to wonder what kind of a Hatfields-and-McCoys feud I'd got myself into.

"How Hilda has managed to keep the stud farm going by herself all these years despite hostile in-laws and a son who shows no interest, Lord only knows." Absently Evie stroked Chamois's ear. "After Daniel died Hilda discovered that he'd run the business into the ground just as her father had predicted. She's worked really hard, but she's never been able to restore the farm to its former glory."

"Who runs it now?"

"Haven't you been listening? Buck's father, Hank Carpenter. He seems capable enough, in a rough-hewn sort of way. But you see the hold they would get on both the stud farm and the dude ranch if—"

We were back to Fiona's love life.

"Enough already," I protested. "Don't tell me any more. I'm here to investigate this horse business, and I can't allow myself to be influenced by your opinions. You must let me draw my own conclusions."

Trixie could stand the blue jays' taunting no longer, and was now barking her silly little head off.

I pulled Evie to her feet. "Come on. Let's take the dogs for a walk, and work up an appetite for dinner. And on the way I'll tell you all about my adventure with a handsome stranger on horseback."

CHAPTER 5

The Family

Hilda Dorsett-Bragg wasn't at all what I'd imagined. From Evie's tale of family woe, I'd expected someone frail and elderly, all black lace and silver hair, her control over her family due more to respect than to will power. But will power was there in abundance in the stern face, tight mouth, and penetrating grey eyes that seemed to take in everything in a single glance.

She was a large, formidable woman of sixty-odd, with tanned, leathery skin and protruding teeth. Her thick grey hair was pulled back in a pony-tail, and tied with a leather thong. Her height showed off to advantage the blue silk blouse and ankle-length divided skirt of tan suede above custom-made riding boots. Despite her imposing appearance, there was about her an air of long suffering, though the only reminder of her stroke was her reliance on an ebony walking stick topped with a silver horse's head that at this moment was propped against the worn leather couch on which she sat. At her feet lay a diminutive, near-hairless Yorkshire terrier.

"Excuse my not getting up," she said, extending a heavily ringed hand when Evie introduced us. Her voice was deep, with the slightest trace of an English accent. "Thank you for agreeing to come. Evelyn speaks very highly of your talents with animals." This last was delivered with a knowing nod of her head.

Her eyes searched my face and seemed to find me wanting. What had she expected? Someone who would fit in with her horsey set, step in, and immediately solve the problem?

My sense that her courtesy was purely for Evie's benefit was reinforced when she said, "You sounded younger over the telephone." I could hear the disapproval in her tone.

Evie made an attempt to lift the mood that seemed to have enveloped us. "Hilda's the only one of my crowd who uses my full name," she said. "Makes me feel like I'm back in England. Mother never called me anything else. Hilda and my mother were cousins, you know."

I nodded my acknowledgement of the fact, as she continued, "Oh, there's the drinks man. I'll leave you two to chat. Would you believe they actually have Pimm's here?"

I had no reason to believe otherwise. I was sure our hostess, being of English descent, would maintain a cellar well stocked with all the British favourites, including Pimm's. But before I could say as much, Evie was gone in a waft of expensive perfume to the end of the room where a tubby man in a white shirt and bolo tie had just taken his place behind the bar.

Dress was uniformly jeans and long-sleeved shirts for the men, and with rare exceptions (Evie being one), variations on the denim-skirt-and-blouse theme for the women. Evie was her impeccably elegant self in a short black georgette cocktail dress, a diamante clip fastening her blond hair to one side.

"Make yourself as smart as possible," she'd said to me as we got ready earlier that evening. Her tone implied I might not be up to the challenge. She was forever making expensive and unsuitable suggestions for my wardrobe, her choices invariably being wildly inappropriate for my lifestyle, not to mention my budget. The directive was not without its perils. I had brought with me only one dinner dress, an ankle-length long-sleeved black knit sheath with a bird-embroidered vest, and one pair of heels, my black sandals.

"I thought you said dress was casual," I said, donning the black knit with some trepidation, uncertain if it was appropriate to the occasion. I knew I could rely on Evie to tell me if anything were awry. She lost no time in doing so.

"I wonder you invited me at all," I replied crossly to her dismissive "I suppose you'll do." Clearly our friendship was not based on superficial flattery, but on an enduring relationship of shared experiences and mutual affection that overcame our differences.

Now, despite my earlier misgivings, I was relieved to see that I had struck a happy medium between the denim I never did care for except for jeans, and Evie's splendour.

Hilda patted the seat beside her, and I sat down.

Glancing around to ensure no-one was within hearing, she said, "I'll leave you to make your own inquiries. It won't do for us to be seen having too much contact. I suggest you start with Austin Tully, the vet. You'll find him in the stable any time after ten in the morning."

"I understand. But there's one thing I really need to know." She nodded. "Surely your horse was insured?"

"Of course. For a million dollars. But the insurance company refuses to pay. They claim death was due to negligence. When I threatened to sue, they advised me to call in the police. At that point it occurred to me that the guilty party might be someone in my own circle. As I told you, there are certain family members," she shifted uncomfortably, "relatives of my dead husband, who do not wish me well. The matter needs to be handled with discretion."

She hinted that there had been lapses on the part of her deceased husband's family, but other than that first mention of Charles Bragg on the phone, to what extent or on whose shoulders these lapses rested remained unclear. When I pressed for details she seemed guarded, as if she felt she'd already said more than she'd intended. "I mustn't bore you with old family history," she said, and abruptly changed the subject, inquiring about my English background.

I had no intention of letting her suspicions slide, but further questioning could wait until I'd found out more through my own investigation.

A woman I took to be the housekeeper came up to Hilda to discuss a detail of the evening's meal. Whilst they were talking I studied my surroundings.

There was about the place an air of shabby gentility, of melancholy almost, for past glories.

The dining room was large, almost baronial, reminiscent of an English stately home. Two walls were covered with faded wallpaper depicting a hunting scene, across which red-coated huntsmen and tan-and-white hounds unendingly chased a backward-glancing red fox across brooks and over fences. At one end of the room was the bar, and the interior entrance from the lobby. The opposite end was taken up almost entirely with a wide window which gave on to a stone-balustraded terrace. Beside the window stood a massive Christmas tree, still adorned with dusty decorations.

Near the bar a couple stood studying a large gun case displaying an assortment of weapons which, to my untutored eye, looked vaguely antique. Other guests sat in clusters in a variety of sofas and armchairs, some leather, some chintz, faded and stained from years of use.

A massive oak refectory dining table, supported on thick carved legs every four feet or so, dominated the centre of the room. A huge wooden circular chandelier suspended on cobwebbed black chains held candle-shaped electric lights, some of them burnt out.

Directly across the room was a slate fireplace where logs burned and crackled, sending out occasional sparks to a well-scorched rug on which lounged the two Goldens. With a pang of guilt I thought of Watson and Trixie back at the cabin with Chamois.

A burst of laughter caused me to look in the direction of the bar. Evie was batting her false eyelashes at a tall man who had his back to me. Catching my eye, Evie beckoned me to join her. I excused myself from Hilda, still in conversation with the housekeeper, and made my way to my friend's side.

She handed me a tall glass of Pimm's. "Here you are, sweetie. Drink up. There's someone here I want you to meet. Seymour, this is my dear, dear friend Delilah, who's come to stay for a few days. Dee, this is Seymour Hicks, the family accountant."

Seymour had one of those bland faces that are impossible to read, reminding me of talented actors who can take on any role, and with a minimum of make-up, convey a whole range of characters from saint to sinner. He had sparse blond hair smoothed back from a high, mildly perplexed brow, and pale blue, slightly myopic eyes behind rimless glasses. Mid-forties, I guessed. A salon tan emphasised an odd L-shaped scar on his chin.

My opinion that his natty bow tie and loud check sports jacket spoke more of the racetrack than a CPA's office was confirmed when Evie said, in her usual extravagant tone, "Seymour's quite brilliant. He's been telling me how he's just turned a ten-dollar bet into a thousand-dollar win at the track."

Such a trick seemed evidence more of good luck than accounting acumen, but I smiled and held out my hand. "Are you a horseman, Mr. Hicks?"

"I hope to get in a few rides while I'm here." His voice betrayed a hint of nervousness. Not surprising, with Evie clutching his arm like that. "But this is primarily a business trip."

A slender young woman with short, spiky blond hair approached. Stacked-heel boots and well-cut jeans accentuated her height. A white silk shirt open at the neck revealed a long silver chain.

"Fiona, darling," exclaimed Evie, embracing the girl. "Come and meet Delilah. Dee, this is my dearest godchild home from university in England."

I smiled a greeting at the young woman I had seen from a distance on my arrival. So this was Fiona. Up close I observed large, intelligent grey eyes and a quiet strength that suggested something of her mother's resolve.

Fiona gave her godmother a kiss and greeted the accountant with a casual, "Hi, Seymour." To me she said, "Welcome to Dorsett Farms. Evie's told me so much about you and your work with animals. I think it's great, what you do."

I wondered what Evie had said about me. Probably with her overwrought turn of phrase she'd made me out to be something like a cross between Miss Marple and Saint Francis of Assisi. Whatever it was, I hoped that the word "detective" hadn't passed her lips. I would have to remind her again that I was supposed to be here undercover.

Fiona looked across the room to where Hilda was now talking to a young man who stood with his arm around a pretty woman whose pregnancy was very much in evidence. "There's Robert and Lucy. Have you met them yet?" In response to my shake of the head, she said, "Come on, then. Let's go and rescue them."

Her accent was mid-Atlantic: American with overlays of English usage, a mixture of American and English vernacular.

I left Evie and Seymour discussing their investments, a conversation to which I had absolutely nothing to contribute, having no financial resources whatever if one didn't count the few hundred dollars in a CD which I would be liquidating to pay my taxes at the next rollover, and followed Fiona back across the room to my hostess.

Robert was slender like his sister, though not as tall, and with none of her calm centre of repose. He affected a blond stubble of goatee, and had an annoying habit of brushing a lock of hair out of his eyes every time it fell across his forehead, which was frequently. Again, there was a resemblance to his mother, this time something stubborn in the mouth and chin.

He gave his sister a cursory nod as he helped his wife lower herself awkwardly into the sofa. The two siblings did not appear to be particularly close.

"Hi, you two," said Fiona. "Mother. Lucy, how're you feeling today?"

Lucy waved a hand across her face. "Don't ask. I'm so uncomfortable. I had my weekly check-up today. Robert took me." She squeezed his hand. "But if this baby doesn't appear soon I swear I'm going to—"

Hilda abruptly interrupted her daughter-in-law's dire warnings to introduce me. "Mrs. Doolittle, this is my son, Robert, and his wife, Lucy. Mrs. Doolittle is staying at the guest ranch with Cousin Evelyn."

Robert took my hand in a damp shake, as I said, "Delilah, please. Mrs. Doolittle's much too formal for a dude ranch."

Lucy merely nodded and sank deeper into the sofa.

Hilda spoke. "Fiona, my love. Good news. Robert has just been telling me he's going to assist Seymour in the office while he's here reviewing the accounts." She turned to her son. "I hope this means that you are at last ready to take an interest in the business."

Robert stiffened visibly, and Lucy stifled a cough against the back of her hand. From somewhere nearby a loud clock struck seven.

"Saved by the bell," Fiona murmured to her brother.

Hilda reached for her walking stick and got to her feet, resisting Robert's attempt to help her. "Don't fuss, boy. I can manage. Look to your wife. You'll need a crane to get her up."

Robert shrugged off the snub and offered his hand to Lucy.

Hilda looked around the room, as if searching for a particular face. "It looks as if everyone's here except Hank," she said. Then, in an aside to me, "I can't imagine where he's got to. He should have been here half an hour ago."

I began to speak. "Hank's your…?"

"My farm manager. He never misses a meal. It's important for him to be here at dinner time. That's when we hear what's been going on all day at the farm. It gives the guests a sense of how a working ranch is run. But we can't keep them waiting any longer."

Fiona cast an anxious look at the door. "Mother, Buck's not here yet, either."

"He's probably with Hank on business somewhere on the ranch," said Robert off-handedly. "They'll show up together."

Hilda nodded to the housekeeper, who was obviously waiting for her signal. The drinks man came from behind the bar with an enormous gong, beat it three times, and announced, "Dinner is served. Please take your seats."

I found my place card about halfway down the table between Seymour Hicks and a man who introduced himself as Dr. George Kendall. His wife, Marsha, and their two boys sat to his left. My seat offered a good vantage point from which to observe everyone, and I wondered if it had been a deliberate choice on Hilda's part. Evie took her place on our hostess's right at the head of the table. When all were seated there were still three empty places. Presumably awaiting the tardy Hank and Buck, and one other.

Hilda said a brief grace, then everyone fell to the food. The next few minutes were taken up with passing heaping dishes of steaming vegetables—green beans, mashed potatoes, squash ("home grown," said Hilda proudly)—and roast beef piled high, thinly carved English-style, the way I prefer. Nothing fancy, just good home cooking. I hadn't realised how hungry I was. Others made similar comments, some exclaiming how the fresh air and the long trail rides sharpened their appetites for dinner.

"I swear I've gained five pounds since I arrived," said Marsha Kendall. "I promise myself every year I won't eat as much, but the food is so delicious, I can't resist. And as for the boys, well, you'd think they had hollow legs." She laughed at her own joke.

The drinks man served the wine, and I noticed that when he got to Robert the young man kept the bottle at his place, sending for another for the remaining guests.

Fiona and Lucy sat next to each other, opposite me. Fiona kept glancing over her shoulder at the door. Waiting for her young man, no doubt. After Evie's comments about this budding romance I was curious to see him. I didn't have long to wait. I was passing a basket of delicious hot bread rolls to Seymour when a handsome young man in denim jeans and jacket came in and slid into the empty chair next to Fiona. Their exchanged glances confirmed that this was Buck, and I sensed rather than saw their hands clasp under the table.

Hilda raised her voice above the chatter and addressed Buck. "Isn't your father with you?"

"No. I thought he'd be here already."

Hilda glared at the empty chair next to him. "Your mother's not here, either," she said, as if pointing out a particularly undesirable family trait.

Buck replied without apology that his mother had sent word that she had a headache and would be taking her dinner on a tray at home.

"Your mother misses more meals, excusing herself with her headaches," Hilda responded. "She's either displaying contempt for our company or she's a raving hypochondriac."

Buck's tanned face tightened. He appeared to be about to retort something in his mother's defence, but was silenced by Fiona's touch on his arm.

Hilda, apparently deciding that such matters should not be aired in front of guests, turned her gaze in my direction. "We have a new guest tonight. Some of you haven't yet met Mrs. Delilah Doolittle, a friend of our dear Cousin Evelyn. She is joining us for a few days. Delilah." She nodded in my direction.

I smiled and gave a slight wave around the table as Hilda continued talking. "Delilah lives at the beach. In Surf City. How was the drive up here, Delilah? We find that with the increasing development, the traffic gets more tedious every year."

Evie, always eager to speak for me, as if afraid that I couldn't be trusted not to say the wrong thing, said, "Delilah had a most interesting encounter on the drive up this afternoon. She was rescued by a handsome stranger."

"Do tell," said Lucy petulantly. "I'm glad someone's having some fun. We need a bit of excitement around here."

I proceeded to relate my encounter with the unfriendly dogs at the mission just down the road, and how I had narrowly averted a fight between them and Watson and Trixie. When I paused to take a sip of my wine, Evie could not resist taking up the story.

"And just in the proverbial nick of time," she piped up, "along comes a handsome stranger on horseback, and rescues her!" She paused for effect. "A white horse, at that!" she added triumphantly. "Just like in all the best fairy stories. You must tell us more about your Prince Charming, Delilah," she teased.

At the mention of the white horse a hush had descended on the room. Even the guests seemed to sense something amiss. All eyes were turned on me.

Robert started to speak, but changed his mind. Seymour looked to the floor as if suddenly in search of an errant napkin. Across the table Buck put a hand over his mouth to hide a smile.

"Well, Dee," Evie said at length.

I was spared an answer.

Wide-eyed, Lucy said, "A white horse. Did you say a white horse?" She looked at her sister-in-law, Fiona. Giggling, they said in unison, "Uncle Charlie!"

No-one else spoke. Evie, seldom if ever at a loss for words, gave me a stern look and a slow shake of the head. Sensing something was up, the guests looked on in anticipation, eager, no doubt, to hear more about Uncle Charlie.

The silence was broken when from the head of the table came the scrape of a chair as Hilda reached for her stick and raised herself to her feet.

"I will not have that man's name mentioned in my house," she declared.

CHAPTER 6

The Stables

True to form, Evie was the one to break the horrified silence that followed Hilda's outburst.

"My dear," she said to Hilda. "Don't you think you're over-reacting just a teensy bit? The girls can hardly be blamed for their surprise. And as for Delilah, how was she to know she was consorting with the enemy?"

How indeed? Uncle Charlie was undoubtedly the Charles Bragg whom Hilda had mentioned as being someone who wished her ill. It was only now dawning on me that I had unwittingly set this little drama in motion. Coward that I am, I turned for comfort to my roast beef and mashed potatoes.

Without bothering to reply to Evie's attempt to pour oil, Hilda stalked out of the room, showing little evidence of the need for the walking stick she gripped in white-knuckled anger. "Come along, Nifty," was all she said. Startled awake, the ancient Yorkie toddled off after her.

The door slammed behind them and the group broke out into embarrassed chatter.

"Uncle Charlie's a bit of a black sheep," Fiona explained to me, exchanging conspiratorial grins with Lucy. "Mother can't stand him.

But he's always been a favourite of ours." She and her sister-in-law again dissolved in giggles. Taking their cue from the girls' high spirits the guests returned to their meal, the pall of embarrassment lifted.

"You might have warned me," I said to Evie when we were back in the privacy of our cabin. "I really dropped a clanger, didn't I? What is all this about Uncle Charlie? Explain to me why the mere mention of the man should put Hilda into such a snit." I sat on the side of her bed and eased off my high heels. "Your cousin certainly has a short fuse. Any more nutters in the family tree I should know about?"

"Not that I've heard," said Evie. She stepped out of the black georgette and placed it on a padded hanger. "Charles is Hilda's late husband's youngest brother, the last remaining sibling and perennial thorn in her side. He still works a ranch near here. Remember, I told you there's been hard feelings between the two families ever since Hilda married Daniel Bragg. After her father shot him, the situation got progressively worse. The verdict was accidental death, but the Bragg family insisted it was murder and actually threatened to sue Hilda's father for wrongful death. Charles dropped that when the old man died, but the animosity remained. I never did hear the full story. It all happened long before you and I came to California, and Hilda's understandably reluctant to talk about it. But I must say I was surprised at how attached the young people are to him."

"Just as well, I suppose," I said. "There's no sense in carrying a grudge from one generation to the next when some of the parties are too young to even understand what happened."

Evie was still asleep when I looked in on her before I set out the following morning. A mask protected her eyes from the sunlight streaming in through the window. Chamois, curled up alongside her, opened one eye and closed it again quickly, no doubt afraid he was about to be whisked away for walkies. Seeing that I was no threat to his comfort he laid his lipsticky little head back down on the pillow.

I dressed in what I hoped was appropriate wear for a dude ranch.

Jeans, a white cotton shirt, and a leather vest I'd bought in England years ago and seldom had the occasion to wear.

I made my way to the main house where to my relief there was no sign of Hilda. Breakfast turned out to be far less formal than the previous evening's meal. I joined the guests helping themselves from hot plates on a buffet set up by the bar. The fare was typically English—eggs, bacon, fried tomatoes, kidneys, fried bread, kippers and finnan haddie, toast and my favourite Keiller's Dundee marmalade. Tea, however, was limited to a selection of herbal tea-bags and Earl Grey, which I find too insipid for my taste. I was glad I'd fortified myself for the day ahead with my own strong English Breakfast brew.

I joined a group of guests gathered around the bulletin board where Buck was posting the day's itinerary. They were going to take a trail ride in the hopes of spotting the wild horses. After lunch they would return by way of the old mission.

"Such a lovely view from the top of the bell tower," said Marsha Kendall. "I look forward to it every year."

" 'Fraid you'll be disappointed this year," said Buck. "The tower's out of bounds until the parapet's repaired. The old adobe bricks are crumbling. It's too dangerous."

"What a shame," replied Marsha. She wagged her finger playfully at Buck. "Just be sure it's taken care of by the time we come next year." She looked around the group with the proprietary air of a regular visitor with a vested interest in the place.

Through the window I could see a ranch hand loading the day's lunches into a horse-drawn chuckwagon, and I listened intently to Buck's description of the horse sanctuary.

Seeing my interest, Buck said, "You'll enjoy it. It's not a hard ride." He had a pleasant, easygoing manner, and I could see why Fiona would be charmed.

I was sorely tempted to join the party, and had to remind myself that I was there on business. I excused myself by explaining that the drive yesterday had left me with a headache.

I was stumbling through this lame excuse when we were interrupted by an attractive woman in her fifties dressed in jeans and a blue plaid shirt. By her expression I could see that something was worrying her.

"Excuse me," she said. "But I really have to speak to Buck for a minute."

I nodded and stepped back a little to give them some space. Buck introduced us. "My mom, Doris. Mom, this is Mrs. Doolittle. She's a friend of Mrs. Cavendish."

I could see where Buck got his good looks. Doris's features, framed by short, straight grey hair, were kept from being severe by the warm smile she gave me as she took my hand. "You're a friend of Evie's? Everyone likes her. She's a lot of fun." She thought for a moment, then continued, "Oh, you're the one who upset the old lady last night." Seeing my look of embarrassment, she went on. "Yes, I heard all about it. Wished I'd been there. But I hate those dinners of hers, and avoid them whenever I can."

Someone else with an invented headache, I thought, taking an immediate liking to this warm and friendly woman.

But she obviously had something on her mind. She turned to her son. "Buck. Do you have any idea where your dad is?"

A frown came over the handsome face. "I was just about to ask you the same thing. You mean he didn't come home last night? When did you see him last?"

"Yesterday, just after lunch. He said Hilda had asked him to check on something at the mission."

Buck squeezed his mother's arm. "Don't worry. I'll be out at the mission this afternoon on the way back from the trail ride. I'll ask old Scottie if he's seen him. And I remember Dad saying something about needing to check the fences out on the back forty. Maybe he rode out there and stayed all night. If he doesn't show up by the time I get back from the trail ride, I'll head out there to look for him."

I watched the guests ride out, then set about the task at hand: to discover who had poisoned Hilda's prize stallion, the Duke of Paddington.

Following her suggestion I made my way to the stables in search of the vet, with Watson and Trixie in tow. I kept their leashes short. I didn't want them to startle the horses, or to get kicked. It was good to be out on the pleasant spring morning in the clear mountain air. It was still not quite ten o'clock, and I took my time finding my way, keeping in mind the map I'd studied at the entrance the previous afternoon, and rehearsing my reasons for being in an area normally off-limits to guests.

It was Watson, bless her heart, who had given me the necessary opening gambit. The scratch she had suffered on her leg the previous day still looked sore. It would probably have healed by itself in a couple of days, but it gave me the excuse I needed.

As I approached the stable area I saw a sign: NO ADMITTANCE WITHOUT PERMISSION. DOGS MUST BE LEASHED. Even though Watson and Trixie were under control, I hesitated to continue in the face of such a stern directive, when a voice called, "Good morning, Delilah."

Framed in the doorway at the far end of the horse barn, Fiona was hosing down a large bay mare. I made my way along the aisle between the stalls to the yard beyond. The smell of hay, mixed with the pungent stable odours and the sound of horses restless in their stalls, brought back memories of my riding days in England.

"Good morning," I replied as I approached. "I'm looking for the vet. Is it okay to bring the dogs in?"

"Fine," Fiona replied, continuing with her task. "Just keep them close, and don't let them get too near the stalls. Most of the horses are used to dogs, but you never know what might spook one of them. Dr. Tully should be here any minute." She wore breeches, rubber boots, and a white short-sleeved shirt with a vest similar, I was pleased to note, to my own.

I sat on a nearby stone mounting block and watched her at work, the horse trembling in pleasure as the droplets arced, sparkling in the sunshine, and hit its flank.

"Is this the horse I saw you exercising when I arrived yesterday?"

She finished her chore, rewound the hose, and began to rub down the horse.

"Yes. This is Duchess, the Duchess of Bayswater. I'm getting her ready for the big show. Bit of a crash course, I'm afraid. I was expecting to ride Paddy."

"The Duke of Paddington?"

"Yes, the one who died."

This was my opportunity to get Fiona's take on the horse poisoning. "Oh yes. I heard something about that. What happened?"

"I wasn't here at the time. I was still in England. It sounds like an accidental drug overdose to me, though Mother doesn't seem to think so."

"But you do?"

Fiona finished drying off the horse and rummaged in a tack box for a hoof pick. "Yes. Who would do such a thing on purpose? Nobody here. And no-one else would have had the opportunity."

She expertly tapped the horse's leg, rested it on her knee, and began to clean its hoof.

Who indeed? That's what I had to find out. But for the time being I let the matter drop. It wouldn't do to seem too curious.

A calico cat jumped up on the mounting block beside me, catching the attention of Watson and Trixie, who had until that moment been dozing in the warm sun. A grey-and-white striped tiger surveyed us from the safe distance of a saddle rack, while a pair of black-and-white kittens chased each other around a bale of hay.

"You certainly have a lot of cats here," I said.

"Yes. They help keep the rats and mice under control."

I was about to ask if there was likewise a plan in place to control the cat population, when our attention was diverted by the sound of a high-powered sports car. We watched as a red Corvette convertible pulled into a parking area a few yards away.

"What's Robert doing here?" said Fiona. "He usually never comes near the stables. Things must have changed since I've been away. I guess he's here to see Seymour. Mother said last night he was going to help in the office."

Robert stopped to speak to another man who had just arrived in a small pick-up truck with the words "AUSTIN TULLY, DVM, LARGE ANIMAL VET lettered on the side.

"There's our vet," said Fiona. "Have you met him yet?"

The two men parted, and Dr. Tully walked toward us. Short and stocky, in jeans, dark blue polo shirt, and tennis shoes, he had an open, friendly expression, his high colour suggesting a man who spent much of his time outdoors.

Fiona introduced us, then excused herself, saying she had calls to make regarding arrangements for the upcoming horse show. "Mother's the honorary chairman," she said with a laugh. "Meaning that her chief duty is to get other people to do the work."

Dr. Tully and I watched Fiona lead Duchess back to her stall. "Lovely girl," I said.

The vet nodded agreement. "Too bad Paddy is gone. Fiona would have given Charles Bragg a run for his money at the show. Duchess is doing well, but she's no substitute for Paddy."

Here was an interesting bit of information that might fit into the puzzle. I stuck it in my mental dossier for future reference. For the time being I intended to play the innocent bystander.

I led Watson forward. "Mrs. Dorsett-Bragg suggested I ask your advice about this scratch on my dog's leg. She got hurt yesterday on the way here, and I wondered if you'd mind taking a look. I don't want it to get infected."

He hunkered down beside Watson. "Here, girl," he said kindly. "Let's have a look."

When I mentioned the near set-to with the dogs at the mission he nodded.

"Old Scottie needs to keep those dogs under control. But they're getting to be more than he can handle. I'll have to have a word with him." He stood up. "I've got an antibiotic here that should do the trick. I'll put some on now and you can take the rest with you."

He led the way to a locked cabinet inside the barn, took a key chain from his pocket, and unlocked it. He found a tube of salve and gently applied it to Watson's scratch, handing me the remainder, and waving aside my offer to pay.

"So kind of you," I murmured.

Naturally, Dr. Tully would assume I was a guest at the dude ranch, and I quite expected him to ask why I hadn't gone on the trail ride with the others. I was prepared to give him the same excuse I'd given Buck and Doris earlier, a lie that was becoming easier with every telling. But he didn't ask, and in fact seemed glad to have someone take an interest when, observing that the curious calico had followed us to the barn, I commented on the numerous cats and kittens in the stable area. I was only partially satisfied with his reply that they needed a continuous supply of mousers, so counter was it to everything I believed about pet population control.

Seeing my doubtful expression he smiled and said something about my being unusually concerned.

"You'll have to forgive me if I get on a soapbox about the pet surplus," I said. "I'm an animal advocate from way back."

He was quick to assure me that he personally saw to it the cats were kept in the best of health, and that he did indeed resort to sterilisation whenever their numbers threatened to get out of hand.

I regretted that I couldn't be more open with this nice, friendly man. The need to hide the true reason for my visit was becoming tiresome, and I wondered again just why Hilda thought it necessary.

Eventually I manoeuvered the conversation back to the Duke of Paddington.

"That was a terrible thing, the horse dying suddenly like that. What happened?"

"We're still not sure. We're waiting for a second lab report."

"I heard it might have been poison."

"Who told you that?"

"They were talking about it at dinner last night," I lied. "There was talk of poison, then someone mentioned that it could have been an accidental drug overdose." I didn't see the point in mentioning that actually the someone had been Fiona, just a few minutes ago.

He seemed taken aback. "That's one possibility." Friendly he might be, but it was obvious Dr. Tully wasn't going to commit himself until he had solid evidence.

I hesitated before asking the next question, then plunged in. "How could that have happened? An overdose, I mean."

"That's the mystery. We won't be sure until we get the final lab report. Unfortunately, I was at a California Veterinary Medical Association conference that weekend. But that's what the autopsy report said."

I feigned surprise. "You had an autopsy on a horse?"

"Oh yes. The insurance company insists on it in unexpected or unexplained deaths."

"He must have been very valuable."

Tully nodded. "It's a million-dollar policy."

"But how could it have happened?" I asked again, unashamedly taking advantage of his good nature.

"That's what I've been trying to figure out. All the meds are kept locked with other veterinary supplies in this cabinet right here. And the doses are marked off on this." He pointed to a clipboard hanging beside the cabinet. A chart indicated stall numbers, horses' names, meds, date administered, and initials.

I asked one more question, determined that this would have to be as far as I dared go. "Who else has a key to the cabinet?"

"Only Mrs. Dorsett-Bragg and Hank Carpenter, the manager. No-one else." He looked at his watch. I had the impression he felt he'd said too much. "You'll have to excuse me. I've got rounds to do."

"Of course. Don't let me keep you. It's been nice talking to you. And thanks again for your help with Watson."

So far Hilda appeared to be alone in her theory of intentional poisoning. Fiona had expressed total disbelief, while the vet, as befitted a man of science, was waiting for a second lab report before voicing an opinion.

The dogs and I returned the way we had come, back through the barn, then passing some storage sheds to a small building that appeared to serve as an office. As we walked by the door I heard men's voices raised in argument.

"I'm warning you," said one. "You'd better keep your mouth shut, or it'll be the worse for you."

The other half of this exchange muttered something in response, but in a lower tone. I was unable to make out the words.

Suddenly, the door flew open and I heard Robert's voice loud and clear.

"I'll see you in hell first," he shouted. He stormed out leaving the door ajar. He didn't even see me.

CHAPTER 7

Calico Capers

Temper, temper, I chided silently as Robert rushed past me. It must run in the family.

The calico cat had been following us at a respectful distance all morning. Now, perhaps startled by Robert's sudden appearance, she dashed ahead of us. Trixie, interpreting this as an invitation to play, jerked the leash from my hand and gave chase. Alarmed, the cat zig-zagged across our path, doubled back, and dashed through the open office door, with Trixie in hot pursuit.

Watson stood by uncertainly, longing to join in the fun but too well-bred to give in to her baser instincts. With a stern "Stay!" in a voice I knew she would obey to her last breath, I left her by the office door and went in after the terrier.

Trixie, yapping in full voice, was on her hind legs straining to reach the cat, now on the top of a filing cabinet. Jumping over Trixie's head to the desk, she knocked over a vase of flowers, causing the water to spill down the cabinet's side, and slipped on the polished surface, scattering papers in all directions. Regaining her footing, she leapt to a side table, sending a half-empty box of donuts to the floor.

Trixie paused in her yapping. It was a tough choice. The cat or the donuts? In her split-second hesitation I stepped on her leash. The calico dashed out the door, past Seymour Hicks, and disappeared down the pathway.

Throughout the skirmish Seymour Hicks had stood by motionless, his back to the wall, astonishment and annoyance written in equal parts on his usually bland face.

Now, as peace descended, he stooped down and began to pick up the papers.

Embarrassed though I was for the sudden chaos visited upon his office, I was secretly delighted to have a legitimate reason to gain entry. I fully intended to take my time helping to tidy up. I didn't know what I was looking for, but I was in an accountant's office, and "follow the money" was always good advice in an investigation.

"I'm so sorry," I apologised, helping Seymour gather up the scattered papers, stacking them ever so slowly in neat piles on the desk. "Trixie's normally such a well-mannered dog," I lied. "I don't know what got into her."

I picked up a copy of *The Racing Form* and placed it alongside the donuts, now restored to the side table.

Seymour, resplendent today in mauve sports shirt with red-and-green braces—was he colour-blind, I wondered—remained silent. Perhaps dumbfounded would be the more accurate description. No doubt he was also wondering how much of the argument with Robert I'd overheard.

"You know dogs and cats," I rattled on. Anything was better than the strained silence. "I've been chasing her all morning." I didn't want him to think I'd been eavesdropping.

He appeared to pull himself together. From his crouched position on the floor, he turned to me with a forced smile. It was almost as if he'd made a conscious decision to be charming.

"Delilah, isn't it? We met at dinner last night. Sorry. My attention was somewhere else."

My foot was still on Trixie's leash. I leaned over and took it in a firm grip. "I'd no idea it took so much paperwork to run a horse farm," I said, as if devoid of all guile. "It seems such a simple operation." I did everything but bat my eyelashes.

Seymour replaced the flowers in the vase, took a roll of paper towels from a shelf under the side table, and mopped up the water. "Not only the farm. We have the guest ranch stuff here, too. Payroll, of course, reservations, advertising, that kind of thing."

"Keeps you busy, does it?"

"The ranch does. There's not much activity in the farm anymore. Breeding show horses is largely a labour of love for Hilda. It's important to her to carry on the business her grandfather started. She talked about selling after her stroke, but she couldn't bring herself to do it. Instead she hired Hank Carpenter to run things for her. It was his idea to add the guest ranch to improve the cash flow. It's worked well. Close enough to L.A. for long-weekend getaways. He put his son in charge. Buck's doing a great job."

It became clear what Evie had been driving at. The arrangement could be construed as giving the Carpenters almost total control over Hilda's affairs.

Seymour's look turned serious. "But the farm still loses money. Interest in show horses isn't what it was. It's getting too expensive to compete. And the stock has depleted. The Duke was the champ, the money-maker, in shows as well as stud. But he was getting old, and his best days were behind him." He shook his head.

Trixie pulled on the leash, anxious to get back to her cat chasing. I picked her up and leaned against the desk.

Seymour removed his glasses and wiped away a spatter of spilled flower water with a loose fold of his shirt.

"Just between you and me, there's been some mismanagement. Hank's an excellent foreman, but as I'm finding out," he indicated the papers on the desk, "he's got no head for business."

Why was he telling me, a total stranger, all this? It was almost as if he knew I was conducting an investigation. I hoped he would continue these confidences, and let me in on what he and Robert had been arguing about.

As if he'd read my mind, Seymour gave an embarrassed laugh. "I expect you're wondering what that ruckus was all about just now. You must have overheard us."

I tried to look as if nothing was further from my thoughts. "Me? I've been too busy chasing this wretched pup." I held the wriggling Trixie closer.

"Robert had asked me to put some money on a horse for him at Del Mar last weekend," Seymour went on. "A large amount. I didn't think the horse stood a chance, so I conveniently forgot about it. Hilda frowns on his gambling, so I thought I was doing him a favour. Turned out the horse won. Robert had stopped by to collect."

Fascinated as I was by all this information, I didn't want to give the impression that I was pumping him.

I remembered something Jack Mallory had once told me. *Always act as if you have more information than you actually do, so that people don't realise they're giving away their secrets.*

"Poor Hilda seems to have a lot to contend with," I said. "And, of course, she's already lost her horse in that accident."

Seymour gave me a sideways glance. "Accident?" his voice was heavy with sarcasm.

I looked appropriately shocked. "Surely you don't think someone did it deliberately?"

"If the insurance company had paid off it would have provided a nice windfall for the cash-strapped company."

"They refused to pay?"

"Apparently so."

"But who would do such a thing?"

"Only three people have a key to the storage cabinet where the meds are kept. For sure it wasn't Hilda. Tully has the easiest access. So that rules him out. Too obvious. That leaves…" He hesitated.

"Who has the third key?" I encouraged him, as if I didn't already know.

"The manager, Carpenter."

"Why would he want to kill the horse?"

He shrugged. "You tell me."

"Did you tell Mrs. Dorsett-Bragg your suspicions?"

"I thought about it, but Robert said no. Thought it might give the old lady another stroke. She thinks the world of Hank, so she wouldn't believe it anyway."

I disagreed. In my opinion Hilda was as strong as the proverbial ox, and could handle anything except not knowing. She already suspected that it was someone in her own circle. That's why she'd hired me.

Was it possible that despite all her claims of devotion to the horse, she had poisoned it herself in order to collect the insurance money, reasoning that the animal's best days were over and it would be worth more dead than alive? Or had someone else, possibly Hank, done it at her behest? In that case, why had she hired me? Unless I was a foil in an elaborate cover-up scheme.

I dismissed such thoughts almost as soon as they entered my mind. Nevertheless, I still felt my client had not been entirely forthcoming with me.

Seymour, on the other hand, while hedging his bets on the poisoning theory, had been surprisingly, perhaps suspiciously, frank. Why, I wondered. Was he guilty of something I had yet to uncover, and trying to cast suspicion on Hank, possibly Robert, or even Hilda? For the second time in our brief encounter I wondered if he knew of my investigation.

Trixie wriggled restlessly in my arms. I didn't dare put her down for fear of more havoc. Apologising to Seymour once again for the dog's turning his office into a shambles, I collected the patiently waiting Watson, and took off in search of Hilda. I had to find out if she had confided to anyone else, particularly Seymour or her son, Robert, the real purpose of my visit.

I found her with Evie on the terrace, seated at a wrought iron table, shaded by a large red-and-white striped umbrella. They were sipping drinks from tall glasses. Pimm's, no doubt. Robert and Fiona were close by, leaning against the stone balustrade overlooking the lawn.

Evie waved as I approached, and I was about to return her greeting when I was distracted by the sound of galloping hooves. Gravel scattered on the driveway as the rider reined in his horse.

"Have you seen my mother?" Buck's handsome face was bleak with anxiety.

Clearly there was an emergency. "Whatever's the matter?" I asked.

"It's my dad." His voice rasped with emotion. "I just found him. Out at the mission." He looked around wildly, as if hoping someone would appear to convince him otherwise. "He's dead."

CHAPTER 8

Deadly News

Fiona ran down the terrace steps as soon as Buck rode up. Now she took his horse by the reins and calmed it, stroking its nose and murmuring quietly while Buck dismounted. He took a minute to recover his breath, then told us what had happened.

As planned, the riders had stopped at the mission on their way back to the ranch. While the rest of the group went inside the tiny chapel or paused to take pictures in the ancient graveyard, Buck tethered the horses, then headed over to the cottage, intending to ask the caretaker if he'd seen his father. He'd only gone a few yards when he found Hank's body at the foot of the bell tower.

Hilda, who had risen to her feet when Buck arrived, sank back to her chair. "What happened?" she said, her face tight with concern.

Buck removed his hat and wiped the sweat from his brow with the back of his hand. "Don't know for sure, but it looks like he fell when he was up on the tower checking the parapet."

Dr. Kendall had come running from the chapel when he heard Buck's shout for help and soon confirmed what Buck already knew. Hank Carpenter was dead. The doctor and his wife stayed with the body while Buck rode ahead with the tragic news. The remainder of the group was following at a slower pace.

Evie was the first to take action. "I'll go and fetch your mother. I think she's in the dining room checking on lunch."

Fiona, the reins of the horse still in her hand, put her other arm around Buck.

With Trixie and Watson staying dutifully at my side, almost as if they realised the gravity of the occasion, I walked over and gave Buck's arm a gentle squeeze. "I'm so sorry," I said. "If there's anything I can do…" My voice trailed off. Empty words. What could I do? I barely knew these people. But it was better than saying nothing, I thought as he thanked me.

I sat down on a bench in the shade of one of the many old oak trees that dotted the lawn. I was ready to help if called upon, but unwilling to further intrude on this family tableau. I couldn't help but be struck by the contrast between the peaceful scene—the mellowed brick house, the well-tended lawn and flower beds, the surrounding hills—and the tragedy unfolding before me. Birds still sang in the branches overhead, heedless of the sudden impact of an event that would change the course of people's lives.

Robert took Evie's vacated chair and grasped his mother's hand in his. "I was afraid of something like this," he said, shaking his head.

Buck turned on him sharply. "What the hell do you mean by that?"

Ashen-faced, Hilda answered for her son. "The parapet has been in need of repair for a long time. Hank wanted to take care of it months ago, but I kept putting it off. An additional expense." Her voice trailed off and she waved a hand helplessly in front of her face, as if trying to brush away thoughts of guilt.

"Now, Mother," said Fiona. "You mustn't blame yourself. Hank knew what he was doing. He's a competent guy. Something must have distracted him, and he slipped and fell."

Robert shot his sister a sidelong look. "That's not what I meant." He turned to Hilda. "Mother, like I've been trying to tell you. The man had problems. Could be, he jumped."

The disbelief and shock with which this tactless and uncalled-for remark was received registered on all our faces.

Fiona turned on her brother. "That's a beastly thing to say," she said hotly. "Incredibly spiteful, even for you."

Robert shrugged. "I've just been going over the books with Seymour, and he's found some, er, discrepancies, to say the least. Maybe Hank realised he was about to be found out, and couldn't face the consequences."

He patted Hilda's hand. "Sorry, Mother, but you had to find out sooner or later."

Realising the implication of Robert's words, Buck took the steps to the terrace two at a time and grabbed him by the lapels, forcing him to his feet. "Found out about what? You dare say that to my face!" he shouted. "You'd better be able to back it up before you say any more."

Fiona dropped the reins and rushed up the steps after him, pushing herself between the two men, and pulling Buck aside.

Hilda struggled to her feet. "Really, Robert, I can hardly believe my ears. But whatever the facts of the matter, you have chosen a very poor moment to speak up. What if Doris had been here?"

Robert shrugged and straightened his jacket. "Sorry. But it's got to come out sooner or later. And it'll be sooner, you'll see. Think about it. Seymour's been telling me the books are in a mess. The farm's losing money. We still don't know who killed the Duke. But my money's on Hank. Cash in on the insurance, and all will be forgiven."

Hilda buried her head in her hands. Clearly Robert had succeeded in planting a seed of doubt.

I got to my feet and walked over and picked up the reins of Buck's horse. It was a casual movement, but my mind was racing. Was there a connection between Robert's assertions and the argument I'd heard a little while ago between him and Seymour?

Why would Hank Carpenter do away with himself? From most accounts the farm manager had been hard-working and trustworthy, and quite unlikely to have duped Hilda and embezzled funds. Until that morning I hadn't heard one word against him. I regretted not having had the chance to meet him and judge for myself. I had come to admire both Buck and Doris in the short time I'd known them. It was inconceivable that Hank would have been of an entirely different stripe.

Red-faced, Buck was pulling away from Fiona and seemed about to go after Robert again. The almost inevitable fight was avoided by the arrival of Evie with a distraught Doris.

Fiona watched Buck go to meet his mother, then turned to Robert, saying hastily, "Don't you dare mention your insinuations in front of Doris."

Hilda and Fiona descended the steps to the lawn where I joined them, and together we offered our condolences to Doris. Hilda, perhaps in shock from her son's accusations, seemed a little withholding of sympathy. I recalled from earlier remarks by both women that there was apparently little love lost between them.

The trail riders began to straggle in. Fiona left Buck to comfort his mother and quickly took over his duties, leading the riders back to the stables where she would oversee the unsaddling of the horses.

I stood by looking for some way to be of help, and when I heard Doris say in a quiet, firm voice, "I must go to my husband," I said, "I'll take you."

Evie flashed me a glance of gratitude. I knew she'd want to stay to console Hilda who had, at the very least, lost an experienced employee, one who would be hard to replace. Evie offered to take care of Trixie and Watson while I was gone. I handed her their leashes and walked with Doris and Buck to my car.

Aside from being glad of the opportunity to make myself useful in this sudden tragedy, I needed an excuse to see the scene for myself and draw my own conclusions.

CHAPTER 9

The Sheriff

We arrived at the mission to find Dr. Kendall and his wife waiting anxiously. They sat on the stone wall a little distance from where Hank's body lay in a scattering of crumbled adobe.

My gaze travelled from the sad group to the top of the bell tower. Leaving Doris in Marsha Kendall's capable hands I walked around to the side of the chapel where I found an outside staircase leading to the top of the tower and started up.

Another time I would have lingered at the lookout on each landing to enjoy the views of the surrounding valley and distant hills. But today was different. Toward the top I passed the bells swaying silently in the breeze, their clappers muffled by padded ropes. The last few steps brought me to the roof, a flat surface surrounded by a low crenellated parapet. Startled, a pair of mourning doves flew off on whispering wings, mute witnesses to the tragedy that had taken place there.

Almost immediately I saw the break in the wall where Hank Carpenter had fallen, and tried to visualise what might have happened. Had something below caught his attention, and leaning too far forward against the wall, he had caused it to give way? I looked to see what Hank might have seen. In the graveyard below, bees foraged among roses in their first blush of spring bloom. Bushes planted long ago in memory of departed loved ones flourished against weathered, lichen-covered stone markers.

Beyond the graveyard stood the caretaker's cottage. On the ramshackle porch the dogs dozed in the afternoon sun. The cottage door was open but there was no sign of the old Scotsman. I couldn't see inside, but the white horse tethered to a sycamore tree outside the door indicated that the caretaker had a visitor.

A gentle wind blew in from the surrounding hills, carrying with it the scent of pine and roses. By the gap in the parapet something white fluttered in the breeze: a piece of note-paper anchored by a small rock.

It was typed, and signed with the initials H.C. I read it through carefully, confirming that it was, indeed, a suicide note, then put it in my pocket.

It seemed to me I'd been gone almost an hour, but in reality it couldn't have been more than twenty minutes. When I returned Dr. Kendall and his wife were still sitting on the stone wall, where Doris had joined them. Buck had removed his denim jacket and placed it over his father's face, and was now pacing to and fro in front of the chapel door.

The doctor got up and came over to me. He seemed glad of an excuse to stretch his legs.

"Has someone called the sheriff?" I asked.

"I called from the chapel phone," he replied. "They should be here any minute." He shook his head. "A sad business."

"Did you know Hank well?" I kept my voice low.

"We've been coming here every year since the boys were old enough to sit in a saddle," the doctor replied. "A fine man. Honest, salt-of-the-earth type."

That didn't sound like the profile of an embezzler to me.

"Have you any idea…" I hesitated to sound too knowledgeable about such things. "Have you any idea how long he's been dead?"

"About twenty-four hours, I'd say."

With a shudder I realised that Hank must have been lying dead, or mortally injured, at the foot of the bell tower about the time that I was having my run-in with the caretaker's dogs the previous afternoon.

Kendall looked up at the sound of an approaching vehicle. "Ah. Here they come."

A green Jeep with the gold insignia of the county sheriff on its door bumped along the rutted road.

I don't know what personification I had in mind for the sheriff of a rural area like Dorsett Valley. A Sheriff Bumpstead whose biggest problems were poachers on local parklands, or Saturday night drunks, perhaps. I certainly wasn't prepared for the vision of femininity that stepped out of the truck.

She couldn't have been more than late thirties, with a figure the utilitarian sheriff's uniform could not completely disguise, and the kind of cascading curly red hair usually seen only on film stars. Green eyes, the palest skin, with a dusting of freckles on a retroussé nose. Surely this lovely creature wasn't the county sheriff? I looked around for her supervisor, but as I soon saw from the name badge, she was it. Sheriff Anna Banning.

I could tell from the warm hug with which she greeted Buck that they were already well acquainted. He quickly filled her in on what had happened, and introduced her to the rest of us.

Then she was all business. Her deputy, a young man in his early twenties, immediately covered the body with a large sheet he fetched from the truck, then cordoned off the surrounding area with yellow tape. Sheriff Banning got on the Jeep radio and called for the coroner. Then she questioned each of us in turn, spending most of the time with Buck and the doctor.

When she got to me I indicated that I needed to speak with her in private. I had no idea how she would handle the suicide note, but I didn't want to be the one to deliver this further blow to Buck and Doris.

I was relieved that everyone else's attention was otherwise occupied at the time. Doris was on her knees beside her husband's body, Marsha Kendall standing helplessly by, stroking her hair. Buck and the doctor were looking up at the parapet as if seeking the cause of Hank's fall. I was afraid I had the answer in my pocket.

Surprise on her face, the sheriff led me to the far side of the Jeep, where we could not be overheard. I handed her the note in silence.

She read it quickly. "Where did you find this?" she said, clearly irritated at what she no doubt considered interference in her investigation.

I indicated the top of the bell tower.

"Who gave you permission to go up there? Didn't you see the yellow tape?"

I was a little put out by her tone. "I was here before the tape went up," I said, adding, "There was nobody here to stop me."

"All the same, you have no business trespassing on a crime scene." She tapped the note with a tapered pink nail. "Have you read it?"

"Of course." What normal, inquisitive woman wouldn't read such a note, whatever her sensibilities? On that there was no point in being less than frank. But I drew the line at informing her that only a short while ago Robert Dorsett-Bragg had hinted broadly that he, for one, would not be surprised if evidence of suicide came to light.

The look of annoyance on her pretty face left me in no doubt that she was unhappy with my response. "From now on let me do the investigating, Mrs. Doolittle. And do me a favour. Stay out of places where you're not authorised."

If I'd been debating whether or not I should tell her the true reason for my visit to Dorsett Farms, that decided me. She could find out in her own good time.

I would say no more. Get on with it then, ducks, I thought to myself. I'd delivered the note. My work here was done.

CHAPTER 10

Case Closed?

Buck read over her shoulder while Doris quickly glanced through the note, with shock and disbelief on her face.

She appeared to fight for breath before gasping, "That's ridiculous. No-one would be less likely…" She turned an anguished face to her son. "Tell her, Buck."

Buck shook his head in an expression of helplessness.

Doris handed the note back to the sheriff with contempt. "My husband didn't write that. He would never… There's no reason for…" She turned aside, looking first one way, then another, as if searching for a way out of the nightmare suddenly visited upon her.

Buck put his arm around her. "Now, Mom. Take it easy," he said. "It's gotta be a mistake. And we're going to get to the bottom of it, I promise." He turned to the sheriff. "Anna, you know my dad." He still used the present tense. "You know this doesn't make sense." He snatched the note back from the sheriff. "Look. It's typed!" He hit the note with the back of his hand. "Anyone could have written it."

"But who would, and more to the point, why would they?" the sheriff replied. Concern for her friend and the need to ask the tough questions demanded by her job were both apparent.

"It's obvious he fell," Buck continued stubbornly.

"Maybe so. But we have to follow procedure. Once we get the coroner's report we can move on with the investigation."

I had never met Hank, but from all I had heard, from Evie, Hilda, Dr. Tully, and Fiona, I was inclined to believe Doris and Buck.

The tension was broken by the deputy sheriff, who had been on the Jeep radio and now came over to join us.

"Any word from the coroner?" the sheriff asked him.

"He hasn't left yet," he replied.

A look of irritation crossed her face. She turned to Buck and Doris. "Why don't you two go back to the ranch while I wait for the coroner? We'll be as quick as we can, I promise you."

But wife and son insisted on staying with Hank's body until the coroner arrived. It appeared there was nothing more that I could do there, so I returned to the ranch, promising to send a car back for them. There was something I needed to check out while it was still fresh in my mind. I hoped Fiona would be able to help me.

Dinner that evening was far from the formal affair of the previous night. Conversation was stilted, and what there was focused on the tragedy. Staff and guests were downcast at the loss of the popular farm manager, recalling his skill with horses, as well as kindnesses he'd shown over the years. A couple of the guests had decided to go home a day early. Buck would be taking a few days off to assist his mother with the funeral arrangements. Rusty, one of the wranglers, would take his place on the trail rides, but it just wouldn't be the same without Buck, they said.

Fiona and Lucy were the only family members present. Hilda had sent word that she was too distressed to join us and would eat in her sitting room. Robert was "taking care of the family business with Seymour," Lucy informed us proudly. Her meaningful expression indicated that she knew about Robert's accusations.

No-one mentioned the suicide note. I'd said nothing, not even to Evie, and if Buck had shared the information with Fiona, she wasn't letting on.

I didn't have an opportunity to speak privately with Fiona until the guests broke up for coffee, and the smokers, Evie among them, took off for the pool area, leaving us alone on the terrace.

Not knowing how long our moment of privacy might last, I got straight to the point. "I'm curious. Is your Uncle Charles the mission caretaker's employer?"

"Old Scottie? No. Why do you ask?"

"It's just that I've been to the mission twice in the two days I've been here. And each time your uncle's been there."

"Oh that," she laughed. "Mother owns the cottage, and it's Scottie's as long as he lives. But the old guy needs more than a roof over his head, and he's too proud to take money from Mother. He's getting on in years and has a lot of medical bills. So Uncle Charlie helps him out sometimes. Though he's told me Scottie is very stubborn about accepting it." She smiled. "You mustn't believe everything Mother says about Uncle Charlie. He's really a sweetheart. And as for the so-called feud, I think it's all in their minds."

Although there was nothing in her manner to suggest otherwise, I couldn't shake the suspicion there had to be more to it. I was about to press further when I heard footsteps on the gravel path below the terrace, and turned to see Robert standing in the shadows. How long had he been there? Whatever, his appearance effectively put an end to our conversation.

Later that evening Evie and I took Watson, Trixie, and Chamois for a walk before turning in for the night. Though as far as the little Maltese was concerned, it was more of a carry than a walk. He would only go a few yards before he sat down and refused to budge another inch.

Between Chamois lagging behind, and Trixie pulling me ahead, our little group had trouble staying together. As usual, Watson was the only one of the three dogs who knew how to behave. Every so often she'd give the other two a look as if to say, "Really, you two. Do try to get it together. You're letting the side down."

The conversation soon turned to the events of the day.

"I imagine this will have a severe impact on the farm," I said.

"Yes," replied Evie. "Poor Hilda will be quite lost without Hank. She relied on him very heavily. More so since Robert turned out to be such a disappointment."

I debated whether to tell Evie about the suicide note. I felt I'd been an unwitting intruder on the scene at the mission, and that I should keep what I learned to myself. On the other hand, Evie would be extremely put out if she knew I'd been keeping this really intriguing piece of information from her.

I was saved further agonising when she said, "Hilda is having a hard time coming to grips with the idea that Hank committed suicide. Especially since it seems to confirm what Robert was saying about him having his fingers in the till."

"Oh, you heard about that, did you?"

"After you left with Doris and Buck this morning Hilda told me about what she considered at the time to be Robert's unseemly accusations. Then just before dinner I happened to be there when Buck told Fiona and Hilda about the suicide note."

"But Doris doesn't believe Hank wrote the note."

"Of course she doesn't, the poor dear. Who would want to?" She turned to give a tug on Chamois's leash. "Oh, do come along, sweetie. Do you want Mummy to pick you up again?"

"It doesn't make any sense to me either," I said.

"What doesn't?"

"That Hank would do away with himself. I never met the man, but by all accounts he was great at his job, devoted to Hilda, a good family man, loving husband."

"Darling, don't ask me to explain the vagaries of the human psyche. I'm still trying to figure out my own." She yawned. "Chamois is getting tired. I think it's time to turn back."

Sensing that Evie had had enough of the sad topic, I changed the subject to something I was sure would be more to her liking.

"Yes, even the sheriff is puzzled," I said as we retraced our steps. "She's quite a knockout, by the way."

"Do tell."

I spent the rest of our walk describing to an intrigued Evie the vision of loveliness entrusted with upholding the law in these parts.

We arrived back at the cabin to find Rusty, the young red-headed wrangler, sitting on the steps waiting for us. Mrs. Dorsett-Bragg wished to see me ASAP, he said. I'd find her in the small sitting room off the dining room.

I glanced at my watch. It was almost ten. Curious about what Hilda could possibly want at that hour, I found my way to her private quarters.

Hearing no answer to my knock I opened the door and poked my head in. Hilda sat writing at a Queen Anne desk which, if it wasn't the real thing, was a very good copy. The silver-topped walking stick leaned against the back of her chair.

She looked up. "Ah. Mrs. Doolittle. Come in."

There was no invitation to sit; indeed if there had been, there was nothing available, the only two chairs, upholstered in a dusty maroon velveteen, being covered with stacks of horse-related magazines. A threadbare couch was occupied by the aged Yorkie, who regarded me with a baleful eye, daring me to depose him. At one end of the couch a Wedgwood bowl containing the remains of his dinner rested on a worn copy of *Equine Trade Journal.*

Hilda continued writing, as if oblivious of my presence. I felt like I'd been summoned to the headmistress's office for some misdemeanour.

While I waited for Hilda to finish her task I took in my surroundings. Lit only by a Tiffany-style lamp on the top of the desk, the small room was claustrophobically cluttered with heavy Victorian decor. Brooding landscapes in intricately carved frames covered every inch of wall space. The mantelpiece was crowded with knick-knacks. A clock, supported on either side by a china shepherd and shepherdess, held pride of place. Dust catchers all.

Side tables stood on either side of the fireplace. One held an old Remington manual typewriter, the other tarnished silver-framed photographs depicting family members at various times in the Dorsett dynasty. The largest picture showed a wedding party, Hilda and Daniel, I guessed. A small boy sat cross-legged in front of the bride and groom, and I could readily see the resemblance between Daniel and his younger brother, Charles. Barely visible among the other guests in the background stood a short man wearing a tam-o'-shanter.

The scratch of Hilda's pen, the crackling fire, and the ticking clock were the only sounds. The smell of fresh-cut pine from the logs stacked on the grate mingled with the unmistakable odour of unwashed dog.

On the hearth a small spider escaped the heat and furtively explored the bark of a log.

Hilda put down her pen and pushed back her chair. The cane slid to the floor. Startled, the spider disappeared under a corner of the rug. I gave my client my full attention.

She cleared her throat. "Mrs. Doolittle. You've no doubt heard that my farm manager, Hank Carpenter, has committed suicide?" I nodded. "And though I find it hard to believe," she paused, shuffling the papers on her desk as if looking for something, "it seems that he was responsible for what happened to my beloved Duke. Therefore, I no longer have need of your services. We have suffered a severe financial setback, and in any case there's no point in keeping you on any longer." She handed me a check. "I'll pay your expenses, of course, but they shouldn't amount to much, just the petrol for the round trip. I'll need receipts, naturally. You've been staying as a guest of the ranch, so you've had no other expenses to speak of."

Furious though I was—more by the attitude than the message—I didn't want to add to Hilda's distress by showing it. But I thought plenty. No other expenses to speak of? What about the days I could have been working on other cases? How about the inconvenience of dropping everything to respond to her summons? Though, to be fair, that was Evie's idea. Now I was to be dismissed without even a thank-you.

To be honest, I'd found out practically nothing, and when I did latch on to something in my meeting with Seymour Hicks, Robert had beaten me to it, revealing the information to his mother before I had a chance to clue her in.

In any case, the police were involved now, and things would have to take their course, though I had plenty of suspicions of my own. Chief among them was that this entire business had been settled far too tidily.

CHAPTER 11

Murder, She Said

Evie wouldn't hear of my leaving. "Nonsense. You've only just got here," she said the following morning. She was sitting up in bed leafing through a copy of *Architectural Digest*, a black satin eye mask pushed back on her blond hair. Chamois was curled up beside her. "Of course you'll stay on. My treat," she added in a sudden and uncharacteristic burst of generosity.

I was about to refuse, then realised that given a day or two longer, I might yet be able to get to the bottom of the mystery of the poisoned horse, as well as the circumstances surrounding Hank Carpenter's death. Almost everyone I'd spoken to, with the exception of Robert and Seymour, had expressed disbelief at the idea that the farm manager had taken his own life. Even Hilda had accepted the evidence presented by the suicide note with reluctance, and only after her son had persuaded her to his way of thinking.

If I'd needed further convincing, it had come from Hank's wife, Doris. I'd run into her earlier that morning while taking Watson and Trixie for their early walk.

Exploring a path different to any I'd taken previously, I came upon a sheltered arbour, surrounded on three sides by a vine-covered trellis.

Doris was sitting on a wooden bench, reading a letter. She looked up as we approached.

"Oh," I said, tightening my grip on the dogs' leashes as they pulled forward to greet her. "I'm sorry we disturbed you. I haven't found this spot before."

The scent of honeysuckle hung on the still morning air, and I wondered if I'd stumbled upon Evie's smoking hideout.

"Not at all," said Doris, leaning forward to pet the dogs. "Won't you join me?" She patted the seat beside her. She was still pale but appeared less distracted than the previous day.

I sat down. Watson stayed by my side, while Trixie, her leash stretched to the limit, gathered smells for future reference.

Doris handed me the letter. "It's a copy of Hank's note," she said. "Or at least what they're saying is Hank's. The sheriff kept the original. But I know my husband didn't write it. He never called me 'dearest' in his life," she said in disgust. "But the man did know how to spell my name. It's D-o-r-i-s. One *R*, not two. Sheriff Banning says he probably wrote it in haste." Her voice gained the strength of conviction. "Believe me, if he'd been so distraught as to take his own life, he wouldn't have written a note, much less taken the time to find a typewriter to write it on."

I handed back the note. "How long have you been married?"

"Twenty-six years."

Long enough for even a poor speller to commit the spelling of a wife's name to memory, I agreed.

Evie was delighted when I said I'd stay on. "Just until after the horse show though," I added. "I promised Ariel I'd be back in time to take care of Lulu while she's on vacation. And, of course, once she leaves, there'll be no-one to look after my crowd," I added quickly, as I guessed Evie would counter with the suggestion that Ariel find someone else to pet-sit.

"I must say, though," she said, "I'm surprised at Hilda's attitude. I don't know what's got into her lately. She never used to be so, so…"

"Disagreeable?" I offered.

"Yes. It must be the stroke. She was always a bit of a stick, but lately she's withdrawn, not forthcoming at all. It's like she's harbouring a grudge of some kind."

She closed her magazine with an air of finality, and threw back the bedclothes. "That's settled then. You'll stay. But you'll have to do something about the dogs."

At my raised eyebrows she added hastily, "Watson's a love, of course, but Trixie… Well, yesterday afternoon when you were gone, she spent the entire time at the bottom of that tall pine outside the window barking at a squirrel or chipmunk or some such creature. She absolutely would not shut up. Gave poor little Chamois quite a headache, didn't she, luvvums?" Chamois, in apparent agreement, blinked at me with a pained expression.

I promised to keep Trixie with me from then on. I wondered why I hadn't yet heard from Tony. He should be back from his trip by now. I would have to call and leave him a message that my tolerance for dog-sitting Jack Russells in general and Trixie in particular had its limits, and I'd appreciate hearing from him as soon as he arrived home.

"Besides, there's no question of you leaving until after the horse show," said Evie, returning to the subject at hand.

"I should've thought they'd cancel that."

"My dear," replied my friend in the irritating put-down tone she had polished to a high art over the years. "Do try to stay informed. It's not just a local affair. Top jumpers and riders come from all over the state. It's very prestigious. Fiona came back from England specially to compete."

"I just thought that, with the death of the farm manager, and since he was very close to the family, and funeral arrangements, et cetera, Fiona might prefer to stay with Buck. Though, of course, they can't move foward with the funeral until after the autopsy."

A look of distaste crossed Evie's face. "My dear, must you be so terribly morbid? It does one absolutely no good to dwell on these things, though I must say you have an unfortunate tendency in that regard.

Death and disaster do seem to follow you around somewhat. Anyone who didn't know you might be inclined to think you carried some kind of curse."

"Typhoid Mary?" I suggested.

She smiled. "Not quite that bad. But you know what I mean."

Actually, I did. She was referring to the fact that my job as a pet detective frequently led me to uncover the worst in human nature. But I refused to rise to the bait. I changed the subject. "When is it? The horse show?"

"The day after tomorrow."

"That's awfully soon. Maybe Fiona will change her mind."

Fiona was indeed having second thoughts, though not about the horse show.

She spoke to me at lunch time. We'd both gone to the dining room early to see if the *Los Angeles Times* had arrived. After exchanging a few words about the newspaper, with its dismal mix of travel delays, violence, war, and sudden death, and agreeing that the most peaceful reading to be found was the crossword and the obituary column, she looked around to make sure no-one else was within hearing, then said, "Delilah, can I ask you a favour?"

"Of course. What is it?" While we talked I kept one eye on the terrace where Trixie and Watson were sitting forlornly in the shade of an overhanging oak.

"I'd rather you didn't mention to anyone what I told you yesterday. You know, about Uncle Charlie and Scottie."

"Well, of course, if you'd rather I didn't."

"It's just that, well, you know, Uncle Charlie doesn't get on at all well with Mother, and if she knew that he's been helping Scottie financially when she's always considered him her own special project, she'd be upset. And she's got enough on her plate to deal with right now."

"I understand. Of course I won't say anything. It's not important, I was just being nosy. Don't worry about it." Better to be considered an inquisitive busybody than to arouse suspicion by persisting in asking awkward questions. For the time being I would take Fiona's explanation as to why Charles Bragg was a frequent visitor to Scottie's cottage, and why she would prefer her mother be kept in ignorance of the fact, at face value.

I went on to tell her that Evie had convinced me to stay on for the horse show.

"Brilliant," she said, giving me the full benefit of her wonderful smile.

Before we could speak further, people started arriving for lunch, and she was called to join a discussion about the coming horse show. I made my way to the pay phone to call Tony. There was no answer, so I left a message. I had no luck either in making a belated attempt to let Jack Mallory know I'd been called out of town. The desk sergeant at the Surf City police station informed me that he was on assignment and not expected back for several days.

I called home to check my messages. There were only two.

Beep: A woman's voice. *"I was told you might be able to help me get a Poodle puppy. White, toy, no more than four pounds, female."* I would have to call her back and suggest that if she wanted a purebred she should try Poodle Rescue and take on an older dog that someone else had discarded.

Beep: A man this time. *"My cat just got killed by a coyote. How can I protect my new kitten?"*

This one would get my standard response: Keep your cat in and protect it from what humane workers call the four C's: other Cats, Cars, Coyotes, and Creeps. The coyotes were here first. If you want to live in the country you must learn to co-exist with the original residents.

There were no new lost dog clients. This was one of those good news/bad news occasions: good, the pets were staying home; bad, no new business for me.

A group of us were enjoying an after-lunch coffee on the terrace when the sheriff's Jeep pulled up. Moments later Sheriff Anna Banning and the deputy had climbed the steps and without any formalities were demanding to see Buck, Doris, and Hilda straightaway.

"Well, she certainly knows how to make an entrance," Evie whispered in my ear. "What a stunner."

Marsha Kendall volunteered to fetch Hilda and the Carpenters. The rest of us, our curiosity piqued, waited all agog to learn what had prompted this dramatic entrance.

Buck and Doris were the first to arrive, followed soon afterward by Robert and Hilda.

The sheriff got right down to business. "I've just received the autopsy report," she said. "Hank Carpenter was killed by a blow to the back of the head. Not consistent with a fall. We now know it's a homicide."

Doris clutched Buck's arm. "I told you so," she said. She seemed to take the news that her husband had been murdered, not committed suicide, almost with relief. She turned to the sheriff. "I knew that nothing would have made him take his own life. If he'd done anything wrong, and you've yet to prove that," she glared at Robert and Hilda, "then he would have been man enough to face the consequences."

Hilda's face showed no such relief. Shock registered, and something more difficult to define. Of course, I told myself, she must be concerned that a murder investigation will bring more disruption to Dorsett Farms. Once the news gets out it's bound to hurt the guest ranch business. And surely she's worried that the killer might be someone in her own circle. "Who? Why?" she demanded.

Those words were on everyone's lips. They had only just got used to the idea that Hank Carpenter had killed himself rather than face the consequences of a crime that was still unclear to many of them. Now a ripple of fear seemed to permeate through the group as they came to grips with the news that a murderer was at large, possibly in their midst.

Austin Tully, Seymour Hicks, and Robert Dorsett-Bragg huddled together at the far end of the terrace. One imagined them trying to figure out who could be responsible for Hank's death.

My reaction precisely. There had been more mystery going on at Dorsett Farms than Who Poisoned the Horse, and I hadn't been quick enough to see it. Now a man had been murdered. Of course, there was no way I could have prevented that. Hank Carpenter was already dead by the time I arrived.

"No-one is to leave Dorsett Farms or the guest ranch until we've got everyone's statement of their whereabouts during the past forty-eight hours," the sheriff announced. "In the meantime, go about your activities as you'd planned."

She went over to speak to Hilda. I was close enough to hear her inquire about a suitable room for use as her headquarters during the investigation.

I noticed Robert watching them, and as soon as the sheriff started to speak, he hurried over and interrupted. "The games room will be best, don't you think, Mother? Central, large enough. Of course, we put ourselves and the staff at your disposal, Anna." He took the sheriff's arm and led her aside. I could see by the way she eased away that she found his familiarity unwelcome.

"Anything you need, just come to me," he continued. "I'd rather you didn't bother Mother any more than necessary. She's not in the best of health."

"I'm quite fit enough to entertain two more guests, Robert," Hilda said imperiously. "Who do you think has been taking care of the business all the time you've been throwing your money away at the track?"

Distancing herself from their unseemly discord, Anna turned and raised her voice above the chatter. "One more thing. Now that we have a homicide on our hands, the investigation will be handled differently. I have been directed by my supervisor to call in"—she paused—"the experts."

Then, explaining briefly that Dorsett Farms was in unincorporated county territory, and therefore came under the jurisdiction of a joint powers agreement for outlying, sparsely populated areas, she added, "We've been fortunate to get someone very highly qualified to handle the investigation. One of the best in the region."

She turned to me. "Maybe you know him, Mrs. Doolittle. Detective Jack Mallory of the Surf City Police Department."

CHAPTER 12

The Detective

My face burned at the mention of Jack Mallory's name. "Why, yes," I stammered. "I believe I have met him on occasion."

What was the matter with me? Why was I embarrassed to admit that Mallory and I had a relationship, that we were "seeing each other" as they say? Though neither really described whatever it was between us. Why couldn't I just say that we were friends? On the other hand, why should I say anything at all? I like to think that it is my inborn English reserve that makes me reluctant to air my personal business to a group of strangers. This characteristic had landed me in difficulties before when I wasn't entirely forthcoming. Was it going to happen again?

Evie cast me a knowing look. She was probably thinking the same thing.

And what would be Jack's reaction on finding me here? I knew him well enough to believe he wouldn't be pleased. He'd regard my presence as at best a distraction, and at worst, and more likely, an unwelcome complication to his investigation. But I had every right to be here, and maybe he'd be glad to see me.

I didn't have to wait long to find out. We were still lingering over our coffee when he arrived.

Though I like to think that I have long since grown out of such things, I must admit to a little heartbeat-skipping as I watched him approach across the lawn. But I told myself that it was merely apprehension about his reaction on seeing me there.

In his late fifties, Jack Mallory was still extremely good-looking, even if a bit on the heavy side. About five eleven; his thick grey hair a little longer than one might have considered appropriate for a policeman. Bushy eyebrows over intelligent blue-grey eyes. Not athletic, though he could move fast enough when a villain was within his reach. His tan was the result of long hours spent outdoors bird-watching. Always well-dressed, today he wore a dark blue blazer with grey slacks, eggshell blue shirt, and a blue-and-grey plaid tie.

He was forewarned of my presence by the exuberant greeting he received from Watson and Trixie. If it had been only one or the other of them he might not have tumbled to the fact that they were mine. But there was no mistaking that combination. As he paused to pet them, his eyes ranged the terrace for me, briefly connected with mine, then moved on. Spotting Sheriff Banning he made directly for her. I was somewhat taken aback to see him greet her like an old friend, first grasping her hand, then giving her a brief hug. They were well acquainted then. The sheriff in turn introduced him to the others. When they got to me, though forewarned, Mallory was still unable to completely conceal his surprise at finding me there.

"Del..." He immediately corrected himself, putting me on notice that I was to keep my distance. "Ms. Doolittle. This is a surprise."

Though a little hurt by the formality, I took my cue from him, mumbling something about it being a small world, Detective Mallory.

Evie, who had been watching my discomfort with amusement, came to my rescue. "Detective Mallory. How nice to see you again. Delilah and I are here for the horse show."

"Mrs. Cavendish. How are you?" As we'd become better acquainted, Mallory had come to appreciate, if not always to fully understand, the special bond between Evie and myself, and had made an effort to overlook her sometimes annoyingly superior attitude.

Anna Banning saved us further embarrassment by escorting Mallory to meet the rest of the group. With quiet authority he immediately put everyone at ease. I had come to recognise that his low-key approach, calculated or not, had the desired effect of leading people to say more than they might have intended. Already he was charming Hilda, admiring the house and the farm, and talking about their shared background. Like the Dorsetts, his family was originally from England's West Country.

Hard on Mallory's heels came Sergeant William Offley, "Old Huff and Puff," as Tony called him. Tall, heavily built, Offley seemed to have more body than he knew what to do with, though I'd had to revise my initial labelling of him as a graceless oaf. Not for nothing had Mallory chosen him as his right-hand man. They worked well together, Mallory's brilliant flashes of insight and deductive reasoning often the result of Bill Offley's more tedious legwork. Like the bloodhound he resembled, once given the scent he would never give up the chase.

His jaw dropped in disbelief when he saw first me, then Evie. He and Evie had had their run-ins in the past.

Now at Mallory's request he began to collect names and addresses of the assembled guests and staff, informing them they would be interviewed individually in due course, and until that time they were not to leave the area.

It was early evening before I had a chance to speak with Mallory in private. I came across him while walking Watson and Trixie. He had his field glasses trained on an upper branch of a pine tree and did not immediately see me.

"A suspect at large?" I asked.

He smiled. "I'm not sure, but I think it's a red crossbill." He offered me the glasses. "Want to take a look?"

"No thanks. I'll pass." I didn't want to risk another blue-footed booby incident. "I think you'll have better luck at the bird sanctuary a few miles back down the road."

He nodded. "Oh, yes. I passed it on the way here, but no time to stop." He put the glasses back in the case, methodically, as he did everything, winding the strap neatly around the nose piece before placing them in the leather case. He clearly had something on his mind, and true to form, got right to the point.

"Are you going to tell me what you're really doing here? And don't give me that b.s. about the horse show. You've always claimed to have an aversion to using animals for profit. Exploitation, isn't that what you call it?"

His slightly possessive tone annoyed me, and I fell silent.

He gave me a penetrating stare. "You know, Delilah, a quick call to say you were leaving town would have been appreciated."

So it was to be Delilah in private, and Ms. Doolittle in public, was it?

I tried not to let my annoyance show. "I called a little while ago, but the desk sergeant said you were on assignment. I had no idea you were on your way here."

It seemed we were getting off on the wrong foot again. While an explanation was no doubt called for, it was irritating that he seemed to think he was entitled to one. I refused to feel obliged to explain myself to someone who not only had made no commitment, but apparently was embarrassed to acknowledge our relationship to the public in general and to the lovely Sheriff Anna in particular.

Nevertheless, explain I did. After a fashion.

"I got this last-minute call from Evie. She asked me to come for the horse show and to meet her godchild, Fiona Dorsett-Bragg. I hadn't seen Evie for a while, and it was a quick drive. Also, she thought I might be of help to Hilda in the matter of the suspicious death of one of the horses." I watched his face to see how he was taking these half truths. So far, so good. "But no-one else here knows, other than Evie and Hilda, that I'm a P.I." His expression turned quizzical. "Okay," I admitted. "A pet detective."

He nodded. I could tell he was trying not to laugh. "Now tell me the truth," he said. "What are you really doing here?"

"All right. I admit it. Hilda hired me to investigate the horse poisoning." My voice sounded defensive, as well it might, confronted with such a question.

His look turned serious. "And what have you found out?"

"Not a lot. And now it's all been eclipsed by Hank Carpenter's death."

"And what's your opinion on that?"

"At first, before the autopsy report, people were pretty equally divided between the suicide and accident theories. Mrs. Dorsett-Bragg was convinced he killed himself in remorse over poisoning the horse and embezzling farm funds. So she considered the case closed and gave me my walking papers. But Evie asked me to stay on for the horse show." I paused for breath. "That part's a fact. She really wants me to stay." He nodded and I continued. "But not everyone's buying the homicide theory. Some still think it was suicide."

We turned to walk back to the house. "Oh. Who?"

"Seymour Hicks, for one. He's the accountant. And Robert, Hilda's son. They're the ones who convinced her that it was suicide. They claim to have evidence that Carpenter was on the fiddle."

A fallen tree branch blocked our path, and I stopped talking while attempting to step over it. Trixie, however, chose to go under it, causing me to lose my balance. Mallory put his hand under my arm to steady me, and left it there as we continued until, turning a bend in the path, we met Rusty. I had a telephone call, he said.

Fearing it was Ariel calling to tell me that, worst fears realised, Hobo had picked the lock on the doggie door and eaten Dolly for dinner, I excused myself from Mallory, hurried over to the lobby, and picked up the telephone.

It was with relief that I heard Tony's voice.

"Hallo, luv, it's me, your old pal Tony. Just got in from Down Under, and got your message. I'll be there tomorrow to pick up me dog."

"It can't be too soon. She's really been a little terror. Worse than usual. I think it's the country air. The smells are driving her crazy."

He ignored the criticism of his pride and joy, and said, "What are you doing there, any old 'ow? 'aving an 'oliday?"

"No. I've been working. A horse poisoning case."

"Somebody been nobbling, 'ave they?"

"No. Not a racehorse. A show horse. It's… Oh, you'll find out when you get here."

I gave him directions.

He must have noticed the stress in my voice, for he said, "Everything all right, luv?"

"It's complicated. There's been an accident. Worse. Someone's dead. At first everyone thought it was suicide. But now the sheriff says it's murder, and, well, to cut a very long story short, Mallory's here."

"Blimey. Sounds like you've landed yourself in it good and proper then. Not to worry. Tony's on his way. Your troubles'll soon be over."

CHAPTER 13

Any Questions?

At lunch the next day Sergeant Offley informed us that we were to remain in the dining room until called to the games room, now the command post, for questioning.

His heavy features set in stern lines, Offley flipped open his notebook slowly and deliberately. "We'll take you in alphabetical order." He looked around the room to make sure that we were all paying attention. "That means we'll start with the *A*'s and work our way through to the *Z*'s."

I was a bit put out to be included in the interrogation, but realised on reflection that Mallory would have to observe the formalities if only for the sheriff's benefit. Even though I'd told him almost everything I knew when we'd spoken the previous evening, he could hardly make an exception in my case, especially if Anna remained ignorant of our friendship. And judging from the "Ms. Doolittle" appellation, I was sure he hadn't mentioned it to her. Never mind that he knew me well, knew also that I had never met any of the Dorsett Farms people prior to my visit here, he nevertheless treated me, as I'm sure he did every other individual he interviewed that day, as a possible suspect.

Perhaps I should have been prepared for this by Evie, who had preceded me to the games room.

"Your turn for the thumb screws, sweetie. Though I don't know what your Detective Mallory expects to be able to wring out of either one of us," she said when she returned to the dining room after being given "the third degree" by Mallory and "the lovely Anna," as she had taken to calling the sheriff.

I didn't quite know how to respond. Explain that he was just doing his job, piecing together all the stray bits of information, no matter how trivial. Or to insist that he wasn't my Detective Mallory. After all, I'd never given her any reason to suppose my interest in Mallory was more than casual. In the end I did neither, silenced by her remark that Mallory seemed to be enjoying the redheaded sheriff's company "no end."

"She's going to steal him from right under your nose if you don't watch out," she warned.

After that I could hardly be blamed if I found myself observing the two detectives closely. Even so, I was more than a little surprised to find them apparently absorbed in a game of billiards when I entered. I slammed the door, alerting them to my presence.

Mallory turned, and leaned his cue against the table. "Ah, Ms. Doolittle, good afternoon."

Offley kept notes, while Mallory and Anna took turns asking questions.

Mallory began. "Sit down. This won't take long." He picked up his pen. "For the record. You were called in by Mrs. Dorsett-Bragg to investigate the death of one of her horses? Correct?"

Perhaps it was my imagination, but I thought he sounded rather distant, as if speaking to a complete stranger.

"Yes. But for some reason still unclear to me, she didn't want anyone at the ranch to know that I was here on business. Only she and Evie, Mrs. Cavendish, knew the real purpose of my visit."

Anna spoke for the first time. "How did Mrs. Dorsett-Bragg happen to contact you?" she asked.

"Evie recommended me," I told her. "She and Mrs. Dorsett-Bragg are distant cousins."

It was Mallory's turn. "What have you found out?"

"Not a lot. I've learned that accidental poisoning was a possibility. Also, Seymour Hicks, the accountant, told me he'd discovered some inconsistencies in the book-keeping. I was on my way to inform Mrs. Dorsett-Bragg about that when Carpenter's body was found. I'd barely been here twenty-four hours then."

I paused to pour myself a glass of water from the cut-glass carafe someone had thoughtfully placed on the table. "There was no question of murder at that point. Most people assumed that he'd fallen. But the suicide note led some to suspect that he'd been embezzling farm funds, and had possibly poisoned the horse as well. Mrs. Dorsett-Bragg bought into that theory, and she dismissed me, saying she no longer needed my help."

Mallory again. "Tell me about the suicide note. I understand you were the one who found it, at the top of the bell tower. Trespassing at a crime scene," he chided. "You should know better."

"I wasn't trespassing," I protested. "I went up to see the view. The sheriff hadn't even arrived." I glared at Anna. "So there was no yellow tape."

Mallory raised his eyebrows in question at the sheriff, and she abruptly changed the subject.

"Let's get back to the reason why Mrs. Dorsett-Bragg dismissed you," she said. "When was that?"

I had to think for a second. So much had happened in the few days I'd been at the ranch. "The night before last."

"Yet you're still here?"

I thought I detected a note of disapproval in her tone, but I was determined to keep a civil tongue. "True. Evie persuaded me to stay on for the horse show tomorrow. Her godchild, Fiona, is competing."

"What did Mrs. Dorsett-Bragg say exactly?" Anna continued.

"She said the case was closed as far as she was concerned. Oh, and that the business had suffered a severe financial setback."

Mallory looked at Offley to make sure he got that down.

Anna leaned forward across the table. "What other reason?"

"None. What other reason would there be?" Was she implying that I was not up to the job? Bloody cheek.

Mallory took over. He could no doubt see I was annoyed. "You say Mrs. Dorsett-Bragg was persuaded to the suicide theory. What persuaded her?"

"The note, of course. And her son, Robert. He and Seymour Hicks were convinced that the accounting discrepancies proved that Carpenter was, at the very least, guilty of mismanagement."

"What were those discrepancies?" asked Mallory.

"I don't know the details. But Hicks told me Carpenter had no head for business. He also hinted that he was the most likely to have poisoned the horse."

"Why would he think that?" asked Anna. I could see she was sceptical.

"He implied that Carpenter hoped an infusion of insurance money would help cover up the missing funds."

Mallory looked thoughtful. "Why would Hicks be so frank with you, someone he'd only just met?"

"I wondered that myself. In any case, I didn't take the information at face value. It's hard to believe Carpenter capable of such things."

"You knew him personally?" asked Anna.

"No. I told you I'd never met any of these people before. But he doesn't sound like either a suicide or an embezzler to me. And certainly not a horse killer. Horses were his life. Most people speak very highly of him."

"Con men make it their business to be well-liked," Mallory observed.

Maybe so, I thought. But I'd been conned the best of them—Roger, my late husband—and I doubted I'd ever be easily duped again.

I took another sip of water. I was getting hot and uncomfortable. Maybe I was too sensitive, but the main thrust of their questioning appeared to centre on me and my investigative abilities, or lack thereof.

I remembered something. "In fact, if you want my opinion, I think..." I was about to tell them about seeing Charles Bragg in the vicinity of the murder scene on the day in question.

But Mallory suddenly stood up, indicating that the interview was over. "Right now, all we need is what actually happened. That'll be all for now, Ms. Doolittle." He looked at his notebook. "Ask Doctor Kendall to come in, will you?"

I was stung. So that was how little he valued my opinion. Was it too infra dig for him to show interest in my theories in the presence of a colleague? As for Anna, she'd made it very clear that she had no time for what she considered meddling amateurs.

It must have occurred to Mallory that he'd been a bit abrupt. On my way to the door I heard him call out, "Del...Ms. Doolittle, wait." But it was too late. The damage was done. Snubbing me in front of Anna! The man was impossible. I'd a good mind to keep the information about Charles Bragg to myself and try my hand at solving the case on my own.

I slammed out the door, to my surprise almost colliding with Tony.

CHAPTER 14

Fire!

I don't know when I'd been more pleased to see anyone. Despite his shortcomings, not the least of which was his seemingly endless capacity for running afoul of the law, Tony could always be relied upon to take me and my theories seriously. In recent years he had helped me out on several of my cases, and I had come to appreciate his assistance despite his unconventional methods. However, on this occasion, I must admit my enthusiastic greeting was prompted more by the knowledge that he had come to relieve me of the mischievous Trixie.

Hopes were dashed as to that last particular, however, as Tony's intention to return home the same day was, like many a best-laid plan, destined to be thwarted.

But that was later.

His holiday in Australia had done him good. An avid surfer despite his advancing years, he looked remarkably fit for a man in his seventies. The lines around his eyes, reflecting years of squinting in the sun, deepened as he grinned at me now, cocky and confident of a warm welcome.

His greeting was typical.

"There you are, me old china," he said, his blue eyes twinkling. "I bin looking for you." He liked to remind people of his London origins and took every opportunity to use Cockney rhyming slang. In this case "china" derives from "china plate," which rhymes with "mate." The last rhyming word is dropped, leaving the unitiated totally confused. Thus, "apples and pears" for "stairs" becomes "apples," so that "up the apples and pears (stairs), through the Rory O'Moor (door), and into Uncle Ned (bed)," becomes "up the apples, through the Rory, into Uncle."

"Tony. It is good to see you. How did you find Australia?"

"Turn left at Hawaii and keep going. You can't miss it," he quipped. He hadn't lost his sense of humour while he'd been away.

"So, luv, what's going on? What are you doing out 'ere in the boonies, any old 'ow?"

"It's a long story," I said.

"I'm listening."

We couldn't chat there in the hallway. People coming and going to Mallory's command post were staring at the newcomer, so out of place in his shorts, T-shirt, and faded blue flip-flops, when everyone else was dressed in cowboy gear.

"Fancy a cup of tea?" I asked.

"Lead me to it."

I led the way to the cabin. At our approach Trixie, alerted by Tony's voice, set up a hysterical yapping. Whimpering with excitement, she appeared not to know whether to run in circles around his legs, or to leap into his arms. Watson wagged her stumpy tail in greeting to her old friend, and Tony spared a hand to pet her whenever he could get it free from his little terrier.

There was no sign of Evie. No doubt she'd taken Chamois and gone for her inevitable post-lunch ciggie. My after-lunch ritual was equally addictive, I suppose. How people can bear to go without afternoon tea, I do not understand.

While the kettle boiled I told Tony all that had occurred since my arrival at the ranch.

"Did he jump, or was he pushed?" mused Tony, when I got to the discovery of Hank Carpenter's body.

I opened a packet of McVitie's ginger nuts and emptied them into a dish. "For a while, that was indeed the question." I told him about the autopsy prompting Mallory's arrival.

Tony pulled a face. His many run-ins with the law had included a couple with Mallory and Offley. "Don't know as I want to 'ang around and bump into the old Bill," he said. "I'd best be pushing off, soon as I've 'ad me tea."

He helped himself to a biscuit and broke off a piece for Trixie. "What do you think? Was this Hank bloke the type to top himself?"

"I never met him," I said, pouring the tea. "But from all accounts I just don't think he fits the profile of an embezzler."

"So you agree with the cops that it's murder, then?"

"Yes. I do. I think Hank was murdered because he was about to finger the real culprit."

"And who might that be?"

"I haven't a clue. There's the son, Robert. Useless. I wouldn't put embezzlement past him, he looks crafty enough. But I don't think he'd have the guts for murder."

"He could've been working with someone else. Who else is there?"

"There's the accountant, Seymour. Kind of bland, and a bit of a wimp if you ask me. When your rascal Trixie invaded his office he looked like he was scared stiff of her."

Tony grinned at his dog. "Good on yer, mate. You show 'em!" he said fondly, petting her head. "Anyone else?"

"There's the vet. But I don't think he'd stoop to killing the horse. He seems very nice, very solicitous of the horses' welfare. He's been the family vet for years, apparently, and Fiona, Hilda's daughter, thinks the world of him. And he was awfully sweet to Watson after she got hurt on the way here."

"Oh well. If he was sweet to Watson, that rules him out," said Tony, the twinkle in his eye deepening. "He could be Jack-the-bloody-Ripper, but as long as he's nice to Watson he can get away with murder."

"Very true," I said, matching his tone. "But seriously, I think a more likely suspect might be Charles Bragg." I related our adventures at the mission the day I arrived, and how I'd been rescued by a man on a white horse, no less, who turned out to be Charles Bragg. "A relative, but a complete outsider as far as Mrs. Dorsett-Bragg is concerned. She practically had a fit when I mentioned his name."

"The old lady?" Tony put in. "I met her when I arrived. Seems like a bit of a tartar, that one." He stirred his tea thoughtfully. "What about this Charles cove, then? Is he a suspect?"

"Mrs. Dorsett-Bragg would like to think so. She mentioned him when she first called me. Of course, at that time she only suspected him of killing her horse."

"Why?"

"Bad blood between her and her husband's family, going back donkey's years, according to Evie."

"What makes you suspect him then?" asked Tony.

"It's not much to go on. But he was at the scene just about the time that Carpenter died. That was the day I arrived. Then he was there again the following day." I thought for a minute. "At least his horse was. I didn't actually see him. I supposed he was inside the caretaker's cottage."

I started to pick up the teacups and take them into the kitchen. "But murder or suicide, the pros are involved now. I'd have been on my way home before they arrived, except Evie insisted I stay on for the big horse show tomorrow."

I looked at my watch. "You'd better not leave it too late before you get going. Those mountain roads can be a bit dicey in the dark."

But Tony, having had his fill of tea and ginger nuts, seemed to have forgotten his desire to stay out of the way of the police.

He put his feet up on the couch, apparently in no hurry to leave. "The old jet lag's catching up on me." He yawned. "I think I'll just have a bit of a kip before I go, if you don't mind."

Before I had a chance to say whether I minded or not, he nodded off. Trixie curled up on his chest, watched me warily any time I got too close to the couch, as if suspecting I might wrest her from his skinny embrace and force her to take a walk.

Peace reigned at last. With Trixie calmed down, Watson dozing in a patch of sunshine on a rug near the couch, the only sounds came from the birds twittering in the nearby trees, and the occasional rattle of a branch against the window as the afternoon breeze picked up.

I'd just decided that as soon as I'd rinsed the teacups I'd take a book out onto the porch, when I heard a sudden shout.

"Fire!"

Startled awake, Tony fell off the couch, cursing as he tripped over Trixie, who jumped to the floor at the same time.

Pausing only long enough to make sure the dogs were safely locked indoors, I grabbed the cabin's fire extinguisher and followed Tony outside.

It was a sight I'll never forget. Driven by erratic wind gusts and feeding on bone-dry scrub brush and pine needles, the fire crackled and snaked with terrifying speed, following the path of least resistance toward the office and stables. The panicked whinnying of the horses mingled with shouts as people came running from all directions with hoses and buckets. I joined Dr. Kendall, Dr. Tully, Mallory, and Offley in the hastily formed bucket brigade. Rusty and Buck made haste to turn out the horses. Near the stables I saw Tony hobbling from one hot spot to another, wielding a fire extinguisher against the onrushing flames.

Through the smoke I caught sight of Evie watching from the cabin porch, a look of terror on her face. And something else. Could it be guilt? Had Buck's worst fears been realised? I was fairly sure that she'd been smoking in her secret arbour. That she might be responsible for this tragedy didn't bear contemplating.

There was a sudden shout of "Watch out! Get back, everyone!" as the wooden buildings bordering the stables burst into flames so fierce it was impossible for anyone to get close enough to attempt to extinguish them. The stables would be next. Then, just at that moment when saving the horses seemed a hopeless cause, the winds shifted again, and as suddenly as they had sprung up, died down.

Thanks to the changing winds and the quick actions of so many, the fire was snuffed out before it reached the stables, though the office buildings were completely destroyed.

As the smoke cleared and folk set about cleaning up, I noticed that Tony looked quite done in. I was about to give him my arm to help him back to the cabin when Dr. Kendall approached us.

"Better let me have a look at that ankle," he said.

Hilda, who had been watching anxiously from the porch of a nearby cabin, now joined us. "Why Mr. Tipton, I believe you're hurt," she said.

Tony, always one to make the most out of any situation, wasn't about to let on that he'd hurt his ankle falling off the couch.

"It's nothing," he said, wincing with pain as the doctor felt the ankle.

Hilda put her arm around Tony's shoulder. "You saved my horses," she said. "Come back to the house. You'll be more comfortable there."

Tony weakly murmured something about having to get back to Surf City that evening.

"Nonsense," declared Hilda. "You're in no state to drive." She had obviously taken a fancy to him and wouldn't hear of him leaving. "I insist that you stay here as my personal guest until you have completely recovered," she said. "Here, you can use my cane, dear."

There was no question that a major tragedy had been averted, though I was equally certain that it could have been accomplished without Tony's help. But Hilda had declared him the hero of the hour, and I knew him well enough to know that he wouldn't deny it.

My last sight of Tony that evening was as he hobbled along, leaning heavily on Hilda's horse's-head cane, Dr. Kendall on one side of him, Rusty on the other, with Hilda fussing as she led the way to her private sitting room. Bringing up the rear was a smug-looking Jack Russell terrier, taking precedence over a confused and ancient Yorkie.

CHAPTER 15

The Invalid Invalid

I found Tony the next day, enthroned like a minor sultan on the couch in Hilda's private sitting room, the couch now looking considerably more comfortable with the addition of several pillows and a comforter. A fire burned low in the grate. Newspapers and magazines, and a bowl of fruit were near at hand. One of the side tables had been drawn close to the couch, the photographs replaced with a tray bearing the remains of what had obviously been a hearty breakfast. Trixie, curled up on the comforter, appeared to be enjoying the life of Riley quite as much as her master, and snarled any time the displaced Nifty approached.

I was not disposed to be sympathetic to either one of them. "Comfy, are we?"

Tony put down the magazine he'd been reading. "Mustn't grumble."

Mustn't grumble indeed. "I should think not. You're like a cat. You always land on your feet."

He wasn't going to let me get away with that. With Tony you have to be prepared to take as good as you give.

He look me up and down slowly. "Where're you off to in that

rig-out, then?" he mocked. "Never seen you in a titfer before, neither." He referred to my hat (tit for tat).

"I'm going to the horse show."

"You watch you don't scare them 'orses," he kidded.

The same thought had crossed my mind. "It was Evie's idea," I said in a defensive tone.

Earlier that morning I'd returned from walking Watson to find Evie in a frenzy of preparation for the horse show. Not a square inch of space remained on the bathroom counter, covered with make-up jars and creams. A curling iron perched precariously on the edge of the wash basin. Several outfits, each with matching shoes and purse, were strewn across her bed.

"Oh there you are," she greeted. "Did you forget about the show? You must hurry to get ready."

"There's plenty of time," I protested. "It doesn't start 'til eleven. Anyway, I thought I'd go as I am. No need to dress up, surely?"

Evie shook her head. "How long have you had that old thing?"

I looked down at my faded brown cardigan. The early morning had been cool, with a stiff breeze blowing. "What, this?" I said airily. "At least ten years. It's pure wool and so cosy, perfect for these chilly mornings. I shall wear it until it falls off," I added defiantly.

"Which won't be long by the look of it," said my friend.

"Besides," I added, "it has sentimental value. Great-aunt Nell knitted it for me."

"One can take sentiment too far," came the swift rebuke.

After a cursory inspection of my wardrobe, Evie deemed I had nothing suitable to wear to the big event, which apparently was as much a garden party as a competition.

"You didn't tell me to bring anything dressy," I reminded her.

"Not to worry." She ruffled through the clothes on the bed. "There must be something here that will do."

Indeed there were several items suitable for the occasion, but nothing that would fit me, Evie being a good four inches taller, and several pounds heavier than I.

I was all for either giving the show a miss, or going in my jeans and T-shirt. But since neither of these options was acceptable to Evie, I resigned myself to the inevitability of her choice, finally settling on a multi-coloured floral skirt which had to be hitched up a couple of inches around my waist and secured with a belt. We agreed that it went quite well with the green silk shirt I'd brought with me, but the black high-heeled sandals I'd worn with the dinner dress would have to serve, Evie having refused to consider my tennies suitable.

Contemplating the result with all the seriousness one might expect in preparing for a Buckingham Palace garden party, Evie declared the result to be not half-bad. "It's quite youthful. You look like a country-western bridesmaid."

That was exactly what I'd been afraid of. But as I had nothing else to wear it was pointless to argue further.

But Evie still wasn't satisfied, piling on the agony with, "Too bad about your hair."

My hands flew to my head, half expecting to find I had suddenly gone bald. But a quick glance in the mirror told me that the wind had rendered my mop even more unruly than usual.

Reaching to the top shelf of the closet, Evie pulled down a hat box from which she selected a green straw trimmed with a multi-coloured floral confection of a type and colour nature had never devised.

At this I put my foot down. "I am not wearing that," I declared flatly.

"Why ever not? It's charming."

I was saved further aggravation by Fiona who at that moment stopped by to tell us that the van would be leaving promptly at ten-thirty to take us to the show. We had been so busy arguing we hadn't heard her knock, and she entered the room to hear the last of our conversation.

"Here, try this," she offered, removing her western-style cowboy hat, a natural straw, with a simple yellow ribbon band. "I have others back at the house."

Though I remained unconvinced that the final ensemble conveyed quite the elegance Evie had in mind, we were running out of time and options, and we agreed it would have to do.

So Tony's remarks were not entirely uncalled-for. If, however, he had any further comments on my outfit, he mercifully kept them to himself. It seemed he had something else on his mind.

"You know what you were saying yesterday? About the murder an' all? Well, I've bin 'aving a think."

"Hope you didn't strain yourself."

"Don't get sarky now, or I won't tell you."

"By all means, let's hear it."

He indicated the horse journal he'd been reading when I walked in. "There's an article in here about insurance. Did you know that some of these 'orses are insured for millions of dollars?"

"Yes. Hilda told me as much."

"Makes yer think, don't it?"

"About what, exactly?"

"If that ain't what's at the bottom of all this. The insurance money. How much do you reckon that there 'orse of Hilda's was insured for?"

"The Duke of Paddington? Dr. Tully, the vet, said a million. But Hilda says the insurance company refuses to pay off, claiming that death was due to negligence. She couldn't get the police to investigate. That's why Evie persuaded her to call me in. At the time Hilda led me to believe that it might have been done out of spite. Maybe a family grudge."

Tony shifted his position on the couch. Perhaps it wasn't as comfortable as it looked. "You say that Hilda's son Robert's a useless sort of bloke, probably couldn't pull off any kind of a scam, much less have the guts to knock someone off. But there's one thing he does have."

"What's that?"

"Access." Tony tapped the side of his nose knowingly. "Access to files, access to money, access to documents. Maybe," he paused for effect, "access to keys." He looked at me as if expecting me to be impressed with this pronouncement. "Any keys figure in this 'ere caper?"

"Well, yes. The key to the vet's cabinet, where the meds are kept, including, according to Tully, the stuff that might have killed the horse."

"There you are then!" he declared with a note of triumph as if he had solved murders both equine and human.

"Where exactly?"

"I'm not sure. But it's something to be going on with." He reached across to the breakfast tray for his teacup. "Who else might be a suspect? Tell me more about this 'ere Charles Bragg." He poured the dregs of his tea into the saucer and gave it to Trixie, who, shifting her position to reach it, managed to spill most of it onto the comforter. Tony brushed it away with the back of his hand.

"Family black sheep from what I understand. Evie's told me some, but I don't think even she knows the whole story. But, as I told you, Hilda hinted right from the start that she suspected Bragg of having killed the horse."

"Why? If we're talking about insurance, then he'd have no claim on that."

"Spite, maybe. Family quarrels. There's a history there that I'm just not in on. I'll have to try and find out more about him. Maybe he'll be at the horse show."

At that point it occurred to me that there was something else I should be remembering about Charles Bragg, but for the life of me I couldn't think what it was. Oh well, it would come to me eventually.

"Is he close to the son, Robert?" Tony was saying.

"Not that I've noticed. In fact, I haven't even seen him since the day I arrived. He's *persona non grata* with Hilda. Though apparently very popular with the girls, Fiona, Hilda's daughter, and Lucy, Robert's wife."

"What about the old lady?"

It was amusing to hear him refer to Hilda that way. Tony in his seventies was probably older than she was.

"Hilda? What about her?"

"She could have a motive. If the ranch is in financial trouble, the insurance money would come in real handy."

"Well, anything's possible, I suppose. But I can't believe that she'd kill her own horse. I don't think Hilda's guilty of anything more than having been too trusting, not keeping a close enough eye on the business. Of course, now that Hank's gone, she'll have to remedy that. Hire someone else, probably, unless Robert pulls himself together and takes over. Meanwhile, she has to rely on the accountant."

"Can she trust him?"

I shrugged. "I scarcely know the man. But apparently he's done a good job uncovering the accounting errors, though I guess there's still some question as to how they occurred."

I took a paper napkin from the breakfast tray and dabbed ineffectually at the tea still puddling the comforter, then continued. "But with the funeral, and the police here, then the fire last night, it's been quite chaotic. I'm sure Hilda's letting some things slide. And with the horse show on top of everything else—it seems she's the chairman, playing the Lady Bountiful—and, of course, Fiona being the star turn…"

I looked at my watch. "Crikey! The horse show! I must dash. Evie will be waiting for me."

Tony plumped up his pillows and settled down more comfortably on the couch. "Before you go, luv, do me a favour."

"What is it?"

"Take Trixie for a tinkle."

I was quite sure Tony could hobble around sufficiently well to take care of Trixie's toilet needs. But he was milking his bogus accident for all it was worth. He must have seen from my expression that I was about to protest, for he shifted position, then suddenly let out a wail that made Trixie jump off the couch in alarm.

"Ooh, me leg. It don't 'arf 'urt," he moaned. "Better get the doc to come and 'ave another look at it."

With an air of resignation, I clipped the leash on to Trixie's collar.

The little terrier had recovered from her momentary fright and was eagerly pulling me out the door before I had it completely open.

"I don't know why I put up with you," I said to Tony.

"It's 'cause I'm so lovable," he called after me.

They say people and their pets get to resemble each other over time. There was no question where Trixie got her cheek.

CHAPTER 16

Fine Fettle

Evie was waiting impatiently by the van that was to take us to the horse show. George and Marsha Kendall, their two boys, and other guests had already taken their seats. Because of the show there was no trail ride scheduled and Rusty had been assigned as our driver.

"Do stop dawdling, sweetie," my friend greeted me. "We were just about to leave without you."

Evie in full regalia was something to behold, looking rather like she was off to a society wedding. She had finally settled on a red silk trouser suit with a white long-sleeved blouse, ruffled at neck and wrist. The brim of her shiny black straw was so broad it could well do serious damage to the eyesight of anyone venturing too close.

By comparison I felt a bit of a country mouse, though my spirits lifted a little when, on climbing aboard the van, I saw that most of the others wore the usual jeans and shirts. Evie and I were the only ones wearing hats, and I determined to remove mine as soon as I could do so without her making a fuss.

"You do look smart," I said, responding to her rather obvious pose for approval.

"I don't wear this often," she replied. "I decided it could do with an airing."

Maybe so. But why for this particular occasion escaped me.

She carried a large black straw handbag, which I knew from experience would contain the various and sundry items without which she found it impossible to get through the day. Perched uncomfortably atop the Sobranie ciggies, gold-plated lighter, long black cigarette holder, wallet, cell phone, and make-up purse, was Chamois, looking even more bewildered than usual at finding himself in these new surroundings.

I was rather envious that Evie could bring her dog along in her tote. I had left Watson with Doris. I had demurred when she first offered, but she insisted she would welcome the company, and that my Dobie was the perfect guest. Calm and undemanding, Watson seemed not to mind.

Evie raised the brim of her hat and peered out the window. "Oh, look," she said, as the van pulled out of the driveway. "There's your detective and the lovely Anna. Don't they make a striking couple?"

They did indeed, grey hair and red close together as they walked in the direction of their command post. What were they discussing so intently? If I was given to self-analysis I might have recognised a twinge of jealousy. But what did I expect? They had serious business on hand.

I thought Evie's tone a little more waspish than usual, and asked if anything was bothering her.

She gave a shrug, and then admitted somewhat sheepishly that while I'd been gone, Buck had stopped by the cabin. "He said he was just checking that everything was okay after the fire, no latent sparks, and all that rot, but he left me in no doubt that he considered me and my ciggies responsible for starting it." She had the grace to look embarrassed. "I let him know in no uncertain terms that he was out of line. 'I shan't forget this,' I told him."

I was sure she wouldn't. It didn't do to get on Evie's bad side. I made sympathetic noises, but since Buck had expressed exactly my own thoughts on the matter, left it at that. I didn't know for sure that her careless smoking habits had caused the fire. But then, neither did Buck. So really he had no business accusing her.

But I did go so far as to make excuses for him. "Poor chap's got a lot on his mind these days. No doubt his nerves are on edge." And with that she had to be content.

I turned my mind to my own misgivings. Seeing Mallory and the sheriff had reminded me that despite Mallory's snub at our last meeting, I really should seek him out and tell him my suspicions about Charles Bragg. But there was nothing I could do right then, so I put it out it of my mind until later, convinced that things would sort themselves out in due course. This faith in time curing all is usually misplaced. To procrastinate is invariably to allow matters to get worse.

Ignoring such inner warnings, I gave myself over to the distractions of the horse show.

Horse trailers parked around the perimeter of the field were the first indication that we had arrived. The annual Dorsett Summer Classic was a benefit for the nearby wild horse sanctuary, and I gladly paid the twenty-five dollars for admission, brunch included.

Rusty parked the van, and we made our way in the general direction of the arena, passing booths offering a variety of items for sale from handicrafts and produce to all things equine.

At the horse sanctuary booth I bought a string of raffle tickets and a spruce green T-shirt depicting a herd of galloping mustangs. I had already deposited the raffle stubs in the fish bowl before I noticed that the first prize was a two-year-old filly donated by Hilda Dorsett-Bragg. This was one prize I fervently wished not to win. I had too many animal mouths to feed as it was.

I lingered by a booth selling used riding wear, and briefly debated the merits of adding to my sadly lacking equestrienne wardrobe. A pair of boots that appeared to be my size caught my eye, and I found myself jostling with two teenage girls for a closer look. They were dressed in sleeveless shirts and breeches, apparently the outfit *de rigueur* for young girls. Fortunately, I came to my senses in time, realising that once my visit to the Lazy D was over there was little likelihood of my going riding again any time in the near future. Yielding the field and the boots to the girls, I hastened off to catch up with Evie.

I found her by the arena watching Fiona who, deep in concentration, was pacing the distance between the jumps in preparation for her ride later in the program.

At the opposite end of the arena was the judges' box, where Hilda sat with several men and women whom I took to be local sponsors and other dignitaries. Behind them was a long table dominated by a huge silver cup, surrounded by smaller trophies, ribbons, and rosettes. The area where we stood and that to our left was given over to spectators. To our right was the huge red-and-white striped V.I.P. tent topped with pennants waving in the breeze. It was open on one side to allow the brunch crowd to watch the competition.

Evie plucked at my arm. "Come along. It's too hot out here. Let's go and find the champers. I'm parched."

I was more than ready for a sit down. The walk from the parking lot had been enough to tell me I'd worn the wrong shoes. I should have stuck with the tennies. Incongruous as they might have looked, incongruity was to be preferred to the discomfort of slipping straps as my feet warmed in the midday sun, and to the risk of twisting my ankle on the uneven dirt path. Not for the first time I pondered the inevitability of the fact that whenever I undertook an outing with Evie I was doomed to be inappropriately dressed and uncomfortably shod.

It was pleasantly cool inside the tent, and a garden party atmosphere prevailed. Waiters bearing trays of drinks moved skillfully between tables set with crisp linens and silverware. Evie had not oversold the elegance, at least among the women, most of whom wore dresses and hats, though some of the younger ones stuck with the breeches and sleeveless shirts. Most of the men had risen to the occasion to the extent of adding sports jackets to the ubiquitous jeans. Others wore riding garb. There was an infectious air of excitement about the place, the room abuzz with talk of triumph and disappointment, competitors and horse flesh. Everyone seemed to know one another, and people moved among the tables greeting friends and neighbours.

Evie headed for the bar. I was about to follow her when I heard a voice call, "Hi, Delilah. Over here."

Lucy sat at a large round table overlooking the show ring. With her were Seymour Hicks and Austin Tully, the vet. I was surprised to find her there. She had seemed pale and withdrawn the last time I'd seen her, and I'd thought perhaps her pregnancy was becoming too burdensome so that she would have preferred to stay home.

She must have read my mind. "Couldn't miss the brunch. It's always great here. Have to pass on the champagne cocktails, though." She patted her stomach. "I get so bored with the food at the house. All those set meals Ma-in-law insists on. And of course, we're all anxious to see how Fiona does on the Duchess." She paused to join the ripple of applause as a rider accomplished a particularly difficult combination. "If she does well today, there's a chance she may qualify for the Olympic trials."

"Where's Robert?" I asked.

"Not the least interested. Never was. Surprising, really, considering he was born and raised to it. Never goes near the stables. Much more interested in the track. Oh, bad luck," she cried, as a friend's horse refused a jump, throwing its rider to the ground. "She'll pick up a few faults on that."

I was glad of the interruption. I had been about to comment that I'd seen Robert at the stables on my first visit there, then remembered in time that I'd walked in on his argument with Seymour. I glanced at the accountant to see his reaction to Lucy's comment, but he appeared not to notice. Instead, he turned to me with an ingratiating smile and said, "Delilah! Great. Evie persuaded you to stay on, after all." His outfit was slightly more subdued today, the sports jacket of quiet check softening the bright pink shirt and lilac-and-green tie.

"Oh, look. Uncle Charlie's up next," cried Lucy.

I hadn't seen Charles Bragg since he rescued us from the dogs. I had forgotten what a good-looking man he was. Today, dressed in black jacket, white breeches, and black boots, he cut a most dashing figure, serious and completely focused as he took the big horse flawlessly through the jumps. I was totally engrossed in the spectacle of beauty and grace combined with the elements of danger and surprise.

There was arrogance, too. And why not? To accomplish such was something to be proud of. His performance was rewarded with a hearty round of applause. He raised his helmet in acknowledgement as horse and rider took a lap around the course.

"Too bad the Duke's no longer with us," said Austin Tully. "If Fiona had been riding him today she'd have given Bragg a run for his money." He explained that in show jumping, men and women compete on an equal footing. "The Duchess is a great horse, a lot of potential, but not as experienced as the Duke was."

It dawned on me that the vet was repeating almost word for word what he'd said the first day I met him, at the stables. That was what I'd been trying to recall since talking to Tony earlier: that the stakes were high in these competitions—prize money, prestige, maybe a spot on the Olympic team. Were they high enough to make it worth the risk of killing a rival's horse?

Having now had the opportunity to observe first-hand how important these competitions and their mounts were to the riders, I wondered if Charles could possibly have been responsible for the Duke's death. This would add more weight to my earlier suspicions that he'd had something to do with Hank Carpenter's murder. Perhaps Hank had found him out. I needed to share this new theory with Mallory as soon as possible.

Austin stood up. "I'm going to get something to eat. Anyone want to join me?"

I'd been waiting for someone to make the first move to the buffet. I'd missed out on breakfast due to my visit to Tony's sickbed, and was famished. I heaped my plate unashamedly with caviar, shrimp, cold roast beef, salads, and strawberries.

We returned to the table to find that Charles Bragg had joined our party. He stood to greet me, and I congratulated him on his performance.

"My horse jumped well today," he said with becoming modesty. "You're only as good as your horse."

There was about him an air of old-world courtesy which, though superficial, had a certain charm—at least in small doses. I found myself warming to him, and was inwardly embarrassed by the suspicions I'd been harbouring against him. Outwardly, it was my outfit that caused my embarrassment. Fortunately, I had removed the offending hat, and as long as I remained seated, the skirt was hidden by the tablecloth.

He asked how I was, and apologised for the rude welcome I'd received from Scottie's dogs on my arrival.

I thanked him again for his help that day, and was preparing to ask him to tell me more about the competition, when he was distracted by Evie who, back from the bar, dumped Chamois on a nearby chair and began to flirt outrageously with Charles. Who knew how many champagne cocktails she'd had? And on an empty stomach, too. She never ate breakfast, and all discretion seemed to have disappeared. She had a tendency to drink too much when upset, and I knew she was still smarting over Buck's accusation about her smoking. But despite being a bit squiffy, she was nevertheless a little taken aback when, the conversation turning to Hilda Dorsett-Bragg and how much she enjoyed sponsoring the show every year, Charles made no secret of his dislike of his sister-in-law, saying, in effect, that she acted like she was still the queen of Dorsett Valley. "Believe me," he said, gesturing to the scene around us, "these days are numbered."

Was he privy to information unavailable to the rest of us, I wondered, or merely expressing an opinion? Though I doubt if anyone at our table wholeheartedly agreed with him, neither were we inclined to rush to Hilda's defense. There seemed to be an unspoken wish not to enter a discussion on something that was clearly none of our business. Instead, almost as one, we turned with renewed interest to the activity in the show ring. Even Evie seemed at a loss for words.

Charles's dislike of Hilda became even more evident when it was time for the awards ceremony. I'd wondered how Hilda, in bestowing the trophies, would act toward Charles when he stepped forward to receive his award. I never had the chance to find out. Despite several announcements over the P.A. system that the awards ceremony was about to begin, Charles showed no sign of heading to the judges' box.

"Go on, Uncle Charlie," urged Lucy. "Go get your trophy." But Charles, seemingly engrossed in conversation with Evie, ignored her, until finally it was too late.

After twice announcing, "Winner of the fifty-thousand-dollar Dorsett Valley Grand Prix: Mr. Charles Bragg on Flying Cloud," and getting no response, Hilda shrugged, set the cup aside, and moved on to the next award.

The waiter came by with another tray of champagne cocktails. Hot, and with a headache fast developing, I was glad I'd stuck to mineral water. But Evie, helping herself to another flute, teased, "Spoil sport. How often in your job do you get champagne for lunch?"

Charles put his arm along the back of my chair. "What line are you in?" he asked with keen interest.

Evie lifted Chamois off his chair, half burying her face in his silky coat, and leaned in closer to Charles. "She's a P.I.," she said in a stage whisper. "And a jolly good one, too."

Charles turned to me, a look of inquiry on his handsome face. "A private investigator?"

I hastily explained that my detecting was limited to the tracing of missing pets. But Evie talked over me, saying I was too modest, and insisting that pet detecting was a cover for investigating more serious crimes.

Others in our party seemed similarly surprised, as well they might be, though whether by Evie's behaviour or the astonishing revelation that the quiet observer had somehow managed to put one over on them, was hard to tell. Charles seemed nonplussed. Austin and Seymour merely looked cross.

I was formulating a plausible explanation when Fiona appeared.

"Here comes the birthday girl," greeted Evie, raising her glass to her godchild. "Twenty-one today! Congratulations, sweetie."

Fiona, looking flushed and happy, acknowledged the birthday

greetings from our group and others at nearby tables, together with congratulations on her performance in the ring, for which she had won second place.

"Absolutely smashing," called a friend from an adjoining table, mimicking one of Fiona's favourite Brit phrases. Beaming, Fiona waved a thank-you, then, turning back to our table, held out her left hand to display a diamond engagement ring.

"No three guesses who's the lucky man," said Lucy, adding, a little spitefully, I thought, "Though I'm surprised he couldn't wait until his father was cold in the ground and his killer arrested."

But nothing could take the smile from Fiona's face. "We talked it over with Buck's mom," she said. "It was her idea to go ahead and announce it now. She said it would cheer her no end to know that Buck was settling down, and she knew that Hank would have approved."

Charles called the waiter to bring a bottle of the best bubbly, and while everyone raised their glasses in congratulations, I stole a look at Evie's face. The proud smile that had been there a few minutes earlier had been replaced by something else. It could perhaps best be described as stunned outrage.

CHAPTER 17

Temper in a Teacup

Evie didn't utter a word on the way back to the ranch. Our companions, unaware of the reason for her silence, probably put it down to the champagne. I knew better. Underneath that quiet exterior, Evie was seething. Exceedingly vocal, some might say shrill, when annoyed or upset, when she's angry she goes very quiet. But I knew that once we reached the privacy of the cabin she would let off steam. I prepared myself for the outburst to come.

No sooner we were through the door than she started.

"Of all the bloody nerve," she exploded, tossing her hat and bag onto a chair, and throwing herself on the bed, leaving poor Chamois to scramble out of her bag as best he could.

I sat on the bed, kicked off my shoes, and rubbed my sore feet. Watson, sensing trouble, came and sat close by my side. As prearranged, Doris had dropped her off at the cabin shortly before our return.

"Who are you talking about?" I knew very well, of course, but I was prepared to indulge her and allow her to rant for a while. The mood would not lift until she had.

"You know very well who," Evie spluttered. "That young social-climbing cowboy, Buck Carpenter. His father's out of the picture, so now he wants to marry into the family and get at Hilda's fortune. Taking advantage of little Fiona's good nature."

"Fiona doesn't strike me as someone who could easily be taken advantage of. She seems a very level-headed young woman to me."

It was all quite preposterous. But nothing would dissuade Evie from her belief that Buck had designs on controlling the ranch and stud farm. She had taken a dislike to him from the moment he got on her case about smoking when she first arrived. Things had worsened after the fire. But it was best to let her vent, and trust that in time she would come to her senses.

"I had such hopes for her," Evie went on. "With her looks and talent she could marry anyone, be anything she chose. There's that earl's son who's just the right age. They got on so well when we were at their house party in England last summer. Remember, I told you about it?"

Actually, I had no such recollection. It was, in fact, the first I'd heard of the earl, his son, or his house party. But I knew better than to contradict when she was in this kind of mood.

"Heaven only knows how poor Hilda's going to take it," she continued. "It's a bit thick, piling this on top of everything else that's happened. It's just one shock after another for the poor woman."

She reached in her bag for a pack of cigarettes. Dispensing with the fancy holder and lighter, she took a book of matches from the nightstand. Her hands shook as she attempted several times to strike a flame.

She caught me watching her and glared. "Don't you dare say anything about this being a no-smoking zone."

"I wasn't going to," I said mildly.

After a couple of puffs she stubbed out the cigarette in a nearby planter and lay down on the bed, putting her arm over her eyes to avoid the late afternoon sun slanting through the window.

"How about a cup of tea?" I offered.

"Oh, would you? That would be super."

The tea seemed to have a soothing effect, and she started to talk about other, less volatile, events at the horse show. Namely, Charles Bragg.

"You certainly kept him a secret," she teased as she sipped her tea. "I had no idea your knight errant was so charming and handsome. And he's obviously quite taken with you. I have to say, though, if I didn't have dear Howard I'd be after him myself."

"The Braggs are not a family I'd be interested in being closely connected to, thank you very much. The entire clan appears to be fraught with problems," I replied. "Not that Hilda and Fiona aren't perfectly sweet," I added hastily, remembering that Evie herself was distantly related to the Dorsett side of the family.

Chamois pawed at the side of the bed. Evie put down her teacup and picked him up, then continued. "Well, one must admit they do seem genetically inclined to rash alliances," she agreed, kissing the little dog on his already pink head. "Hilda's impulsive marriage to Daniel Bragg is what set this whole family turmoil in motion. And of course, her father and grandfather were adamant that the two families have as little as possible to do with each other. Very *Romeo and Juliet*," she added.

I asked if she thought Hilda had ever regretted her choice.

"She's never said so in so many words. But she must have done. After her father shot Daniel, all contact with the Braggs was severed until recently when Charles came back on the scene. Apparently he had leased out the property for many years. But now he's back and Hilda seems to think he's bent on revenge."

She shifted Chamois from her pillow, and laid her head down. "And now look what she's left with. The whole family at odds, she's dependent on strangers to run her business for her. A weak son, whose marriage was not exactly wise." She raised her eyebrows. "A case of having to, I'm afraid. And now here's Fiona, barely out of the schoolroom, declaring her intention of getting married. To a cowboy, of all people!"

"Rashness does seem to run in the family, I agree." I tried to change the subject. "But in any case, I think we'd be well advised to steer clear of Charles."

"How so?"

I told her of my suspicions, reminding her that I'd seen Charles near the mission at about the same time the police estimated Hank Carpenter had been murdered.

"That's all? No. You've got it all wrong, my dear. I refuse to believe that lovely man would stoop so low. And if you're trying to pin the horse business on him, too, well, where's the sense in that? He couldn't claim the insurance money. And what other reason could he have?"

"To put Fiona out of the running in the horse show? Everyone says she'd have had a good chance of winning if she'd been riding the Duke of Paddington."

"What utter nonsense."

I agreed that the notion was far-fetched. But it didn't do to limit oneself to the most likely suspects.

"I'm sure there were others in the area at the same time, who might have had more plausible motives if we did but know them," Evie argued.

"True. The old caretaker, Scottie, for one. But he doesn't look like he'd have the strength to push anyone off the tower, much less a stronger, younger man like Hank Carpenter."

What was the connection there, I wondered again, between Scottie and Charles Bragg? Had Fiona told me, did she even know, the whole truth about that?

At least I'd been successful in distracting Evie from Fiona's engagement. Now she directed her criticism at me.

"You really shouldn't go around making groundless accusations, sweetie. You know what people are."

"What are they?"

"Don't be provoking. You know what I mean. It's all very well when you're talking to me. I know where you're coming from, being a pet detective, as you so quaintly call it. But other people might get the wrong impression, seeing you snooping around."

"Well, you're the one who announced to the world at lunch today that I was a P.I."

"What? Oh, yes. I did, didn't I." She yawned, and closed her eyes. "Well, no harm done. No-one was paying attention."

How would she know? She was busy flirting with Charles at the time.

Besides it wasn't true. "People *were* paying attention," I said. "And that reminds me." I drew closer to the bed. I didn't want her to fall asleep until I had an answer. "I've been meaning to ask you. When you called and asked me to come here to look into the horse poisoning, was anyone else within hearing? Besides Hilda, I mean?"

Evie opened her eyes. "Like who?"

"Anyone. One of the staff? Robert? Seymour, perhaps?"

"Now that you mention it, I seem to recall that Austin came in from the terrace just as Hilda hung up. He might have overheard. Why do you ask?"

"Just curious."

"Well you know what curiosity did. Anyway, that's all water under the bridge now. Don't fuss so. You've no idea how tiresome that is. No-one cares why you're here anymore."

Well, *I* did.

CHAPTER 18

Alibis

Evie dozed off. I was tempted to put my feet up for five minutes myself, but Watson was fidgeting for a walk. And Chamois—he whose paws rarely touched the ground—could benefit from some exercise, too. I changed into jeans, my new wild horse T-shirt and tennies, consigned the offending floral skirt to the closet, and began to feel human again.

Taking care not to disturb Evie, I scooped Chamois off the bed and headed out the door, Watson in tow.

The wind had calmed to a gentle breeze, and after a brisk walk had cleared my head, I made my way to the lobby telephone to call home and check my messages. There were three, only one of them remotely resembling an assignment, though the first was calculated to set my blood to a slow boil.

"Can you help me?" the woman said. *"We just adopted a small, mixed-breed dog from the shelter to replace our last dog, which got hit by a car."* (Shame on her for not taking better care of her pet.) *"The new dog doesn't bark and isn't lively enough after the last one. Can you help me find it another home?"*

I looked at Watson and sighed. She gazed back with a mournful expression. A shelter alumna herself, I swear she can read my mind. Chamois, perched on a nearby stack of telephone directories, merely looked puzzled. But then he always does. I would call the woman back and suggest that perhaps the new dog had been traumatised from being in the shelter, or maybe a medical problem was causing it to be so docile. Would she please take it to a vet, and give it more time to settle in, as her only option would be to return it to the shelter, where there was little chance of a mixed-breed reject being adopted a second time.

The next caller, a man, said his Bulldog had issues, and he'd welcome the chance to discuss them with me. Issues with whom or with what was left to my imagination. I was in no hurry to embark on a lengthy conversation with someone who used the words *Bulldog* and *issues* in the same sentence, but it might be a job. I called and left a message on the answering machine that I was out of town on assignment for a couple more days, and would get in touch as soon as I returned.

The last call was Ariel's reminding me of my promise to watch Lulu the following week. If I didn't think I'd be back in time, she could get someone else.

Suddenly I was anxious to go home. I was becoming lazy hanging out at the guest ranch, too accustomed to leisurely breakfasts, laundry service, pleasant strolls in the woods, lunch and dinner laid on. It was like being on holiday, and now it seemed there might be a job in the offing. I'd kept my promise to Evie to stay for the horse show, now it was time to leave.

I'd been at Dorsett Farms for a week on what had turned out to be a wild goose chase. I had been unable to find out who had poisoned the horse. It was of little consolation to know that, as far as I could tell, neither was Mallory having much success discovering who killed Hank Carpenter.

I'd done my best to stay out of his way since his nasty snub the previous day. How could I have so misunderstood his temperament? But I'd procrastinated long enough about telling him my suspicions regarding Charles Bragg. And my impression from the horse show about the fierceness of the competition made it imperative that I share the information with Mallory as soon as possible. If I was to leave the following day, I'd better take the proverbial bull by the horns and get it over with.

Tucking Chamois under my arm and keeping Watson on a short leash, I made my way to the games room—now officially the command post, complete with a handprinted "Keep Out" sign on the door—and knocked.

"Come in," called Sheriff Anna. I thought I detected a trace of laughter in her voice.

It appeared I'd again interrupted a game of billiards. Anna, cue in hand, her lovely red hair tumbling around her face, leaned across the table to make a shot. Mallory stood close by.

"I say! Am I disturbing you?" I said.

Mallory leaned his cue against the table, and walked toward me. "Not disturbing us at all, Ms. Doolittle," he said.

I would have preferred to speak to him in private, but Anna showed no signs of leaving. Why should she? She was part of the investigation team. Hesitantly, I launched into my report of how I'd seen Charles Bragg at the mission the afternoon I arrived. "At the approximate time of Hank Carpenter's death," I stammered as I finished. Somehow it didn't sound as important as it had when I'd played it over in my mind, and Mallory responded exactly as I anticipated.

"That's it?" he said.

"Well, not exactly." It was hard to be dignified with a squirming Maltese terrier under one arm and a large dog pulling on the other in her eagerness to greet Mallory. I shifted Chamois to the other arm, dropping Watson's leash in the process. She immediately leapt towards her old friend. He scratched her under the chin. She looked at him adoringly.

"There is something else," I said, trying, without success, to step on Watson's leash. "There's also the matter of the poisoned horse. I learned at the show today that its death put Fiona out of the running to win the big prize. Charles Bragg won easily because Fiona had to compete on an inferior mount."

If I'd expected thanks for bringing this useful piece of information to his attention, I would have been disappointed. Fortunately, I harboured no such expectations.

"Why didn't you say something sooner about seeing Bragg at the mission?" Mallory asked.

It might have occurred to me to say that having been cut off so abruptly the last time I tried to tell him about Charles, I was in no hurry to be snubbed again.

Instead, I nodded my head in the direction of Sheriff Anna, still at the billiards table. "Well, you don't exactly seem to be busy, maybe you could use a few new clues to be getting on with." It was intended to be humourous, but I'm afraid it came out sounding rather tart.

Mallory struggled to keep the irritation out of his voice. "We're waiting for Offley to get back. He's checking an alibi."

"Charles Bragg's?"

"No. Robert's."

"Oh, yes. He took his wife to the doctor's office that day."

Another flicker of annoyance. "How do you know?"

"Lucy said so."

Now it was his turn to be stopped short. I took advantage of the silence and said, "What about Charles Bragg's alibi?"

Mallory consulted his notes. "He claims to have been out riding all afternoon, and saw no-one."

"He didn't mention meeting me at the mission?"

"No."

"There you are then. If he had nothing to hide, why didn't he tell you? He can hardly have forgotten." I went on to describe how he had helped me ward off the dogs.

Mallory wrote that down, then said, "There were several other people in the area at about the same time, the trail riders, for example, the old caretaker. But I think we can rule *him* out. He'd never have been able to make it up the tower stairs."

"But none of them harbour the kind of grudge against the family that Charles Bragg does," I replied.

"How do you know?"

He had me there.

Anna glanced with interest in our direction. She had obviously decided to let Mallory handle the interview on his own. No doubt she wondered about our oddly familiar relationship. Was she developing an interest in him herself? If so, I'd only myself to blame. I'd been reluctant to admit we even knew each other when she first mentioned his name.

Mallory caught her watching us. His next remark was not reassuring. "Better get those dogs walked, Ms. Doolittle. See if you can pick up any more gossip."

That this was uncalled-for must have immediately occurred to him. He gave me an apologetic smile and said, "Tell you what. If you want to help, we," he nodded in Anna's direction, "need to keep tabs on the vet. He's being very closed-mouthed about something, and so far we haven't been able to confirm his alibi. I hear he's planning to go on the trail ride tomorrow. Why don't you go along and see what you can find out from him?"

"Dr. Tully?" I said. My voice sounded surprised, as well it might, confronted with such a request. I was about to blurt out how kind he'd been to Watson, but remembered in time Tony's derision the last time I expressed that sentiment.

I gave Mallory a close look. Was this a ruse to get me out of his way? The request seemed genuine enough. But what evidence did he have on Tully? It was rather a big leap for me to go from suspecting Charles Bragg to suspecting the vet, one I did not feel equal to making just then. But why, if I'd been willing to suspect the worst of Charles simply because I saw him at the mission, shouldn't I be equally suspicious of Tully, who, if nothing else, certainly had more opportunity to harm the horse?

I told Mallory I'd think about it. It would mean staying on longer, and there was that potential assignment waiting for me, but it would be fun to go on a trail ride before I left. Who knew when I'd get another chance? And when I learned at dinner that the ride would be going within sight of the horse sanctuary, my mind was made up. The Bulldog and his issues could wait. I called Ariel and told her I was delaying my departure one more day.

CHAPTER 19

Trail Ride

"Cor, you don't 'alf look a toff in that get-up," teased Tony, looking Evie up and down.

Mistaking his sarcasm for admiration, Evie modelled the outfit for him, twirling, and then slapping her crop against her finely tailored breeches.

I had to admit she looked quite stunning, if wildly out of place, in her English riding habit. Custom-made from head to toe, the helmet chin strap fastened just so above a crisp white stock and carefully fitted black velvet jacket, and boots the like of which I'll wager the Lazy D had never seen before. More befitting the Shropshire Hunt than a western trail ride. The rest of us wore the usual jeans, shirts, and straw cowboy hats. A few had riding boots, but most made do with their tennies.

Tony had come to the stable after breakfast to see us off on our day-long excursion. After a day resting his leg, he was now hobbling around with the aid of Hilda's walking stick, and had been installed in his own rent-free cabin. Evie and I had prevailed upon him to take care of Chamois and Watson during our absence.

The chuckwagon was to meet us at Wild Horse Canyon, a favourite watering hole on these trail rides, I'd learned, with its sweet grass and cool stream. One of the ranch hands, a leathered old fellow who went by the name of Ol' Curly, though he was bald as an egg, drove the team, though he said, only half joking, that they didn't need a driver. "Just load up the wagon, point them in the right direction, and they'd find their own way, they're so used to the trail. And the carrot they get when they get there." He chuckled. "You'll be going the long way around. We take the short cut."

Our group consisted of Evie, myself, George and Marsha Kendall, their two boys, John and Brian, and Austin Tully. I had half hoped the vet wouldn't show up. I'd taken a liking to him and didn't feel comfortable playing detective to his suspect. I wanted to enjoy the ride, but business was business.

Buck and Rusty helped us pick out our horses. "This is Bonnie," said Buck, helping me into the unfamiliar western saddle and adjusting the stirrups. She appeared to be a docile, plodding beast, but I still felt way too far off the ground astride the big brown horse.

We set off down the road, Rusty in the lead, followed by Evie and Marsha. I managed to manoeuvre Bonnie alongside Austin, who was riding his own horse, a beautiful black mare named Bess. We were followed by George Kendall and the boys. Buck brought up the rear to keep stragglers in check.

For the first hour the trail wound through roadless wilderness, across meadows bright with wild mustard and golden poppies. As the trail climbed, the joyous spring song of the meadowlark gave way to the lonely call of the hawk. Out there in the crystal-clear air, under a cloudless sky, our recent problems seemed remote, some even trivial.

From time to time Rusty would drop back to show us places of interest. Excitement ran high when he pointed to a herd of wild horses grazing in a distant meadow. "We'll get a closer look after lunch," he promised. He told us that the Bureau of Land Management would soon be holding their spring round-up. "Then they'll be put up for adoption." When I expressed dismay that these lovely wild creatures were to be captured and tamed, he explained that it was necessary to thin the herd or there wouldn't be sufficient food to sustain them. I couldn't bear to think of the terrified animals being herded by helicopter. What would be their ultimate fate? I shook my head trying to erase the images that arose. I couldn't allow such dismal thoughts to spoil the day.

At the crest of a rise we stopped to rest the horses and take in the magnificent views. Turning in his saddle to look back in the direction we had come from, Austin pointed out Dorsett Farms and the ranch far below. The buildings looked like dolls' houses from our vantage point. Near the stables a blackened patch of earth marked the site of the recent fire. Beyond the ranch I could see the mission bell tower where Hank Carpenter had met his fate. If I'd been up here that day, would I have seen two figures struggling, one to the death?

Here was my chance to speak to Austin about the caretaker. I was still searching for the right words when he gave me the opening I'd been seeking.

"How's the Dobie doing?" he asked. "Is her leg healed?"

"Yes, thank you. The ointment did the trick. The wound started to heal almost immediately." I took a deep breath and launched in. "You know, those dogs gave me quite a scare. I'm surprised that man Scottie allows them to roam like that. Someone ought to speak to him about it before they do some real damage. Could you? Do you know him well enough?" I congratulated myself on handling this so adroitly.

The vet didn't answer directly. "He keeps to himself pretty much. I've been meaning to speak to him about taking better care of the dogs, but I never seem to have the time."

Then what made Mallory think he was at the scene the day of the murder?

"You wouldn't have seen them the day I was there, then," I pressed on. "Some of them looked like they have the mange and need treatment."

"When was that?"

"The day before I first met you at the stables."

He appeared to give it some thought. "No. I went into L.A. for supplies. I was gone all day."

He sounded evasive. I didn't know whether to believe him or not. I did know I couldn't push any further. What might he have had against Hank Carpenter? Maybe Hank had found out that the vet had poisoned the horse. But Austin told me he was at the CVMA convention the weekend the horse died. An easy enough alibi for Mallory to check, surely.

We rode together until the trail, narrowing as it skirted the mountainside, put an end to conversation, and I let Austin go ahead of me. Now all my attention was focused on staying in the uncomfortable western saddle. I had been schooled on a small English saddle, where I'd felt much more in control of the horse. I held my breath when occasionally a rock would skitter beneath Bonnie's hooves. But going up was easy compared to our descent. Then all chatter ceased. Even Evie's restless tongue fell silent. The only sounds to be heard were of creaking leather and the breathing of the horses. Below I could see a gleaming stream. Down there somewhere the chuckwagon waited with lunch. I hoped I would make it in one piece.

The horses' hooves sent small rocks flying in all directions as they picked their way on the uneven, dry, sandy ground. I tried to sit upright, but as the trail got steeper I felt as if I would slide right out of the saddle and over Bonnie's head.

"Don't hold her back, let her find her way," Buck called to me in encouragement. "Give her some heel."

Encourage her to go faster! Not bloody likely. I could hardly feel my feet, never mind my heels. I gazed between the horse's ears at the steep, rocky path falling away before me and prayed I would stay in the saddle until we reached the canyon floor.

Then young John Kendall, no doubt trying to be helpful, or maybe in a fit of impatience, I'll never know, came up close behind me and applied his switch to Bonnie's rump. Startled, she bolted past the lead riders. My life passed before my eyes as we hurtled all the way to the bottom of the canyon, not stopping until Bonnie pulled up sharp by the stream's edge, where I did indeed go flying between her ears.

Thrown unceremoniously to the ground, I hit my head on something hard.

I couldn't have been out for more than a second or two, for when I opened my eyes the others were still coming towards me. I tried to sit up. Groping around in the dirt for a hand hold, I touched something soft and woolly. At first I thought it was a small animal, perhaps a rabbit or squirrel, and snatched my hand away. On looking, I saw it was a red tam-o'-shanter. As my gaze travelled further along the ground I started to scream.

The scream was still echoing against the canyon walls when Evie reached my side.

"Delilah. Thank God you're all right," she said. "But for heaven's sake, do stop that terrible noise."

Then her eyes followed my shaking finger to an outcropping of rock and the body that lay beneath, and her screams echoed my own.

CHAPTER 20

Bridled Enthusiasm

Scottie was still alive when we reached him, but he had suffered external and very possibly internal injuries, as well as shock and exposure, and Dr. Kendall said there was no time to be lost if there was any hope of saving the old man's life.

Evie tried repeatedly to reach the sheriff's office on her cell phone, but reception in that remote area was impossible, and we finally had to give up hope of getting a helicopter out to the canyon. Buck and Austin fashioned a makeshift stretcher from blankets and wood from the chuckwagon, then gently placed Scottie in the back. Dr. Kendall squeezed in alongside.

It was a solemn procession that returned via Curly's short cut to the Lazy D.

Although I was game to try remounting Bonnie, the doctor persuaded me that I might have suffered a slight concussion in the fall and would be better off sitting with Curly. I passed the time admiring the old ranch hand's skill with the team, and observing the intricacies of the harness, where every buckle and every strap had its own unique purpose in the whole.

Evie rode alongside me most of the way, her mind less on our sad cargo than on what had caused my horse to bolt.

She did not mince words, suggesting, not so *sotto voce*, that it was all Buck's fault for not selecting my horse with more care. I repeatedly voiced my opinion that he was blameless, and if anyone was at fault it was young John Kendall, and he had not acted maliciously. But Evie would have none of it. She was only too delighted to have something else to blame on Fiona's fiancé.

"Not to put too fine a point on it, he might have got you killed," she declared.

The team paused at the crossroads before turning onto the highway leading to the ranch, and I glanced into the back of the wagon where George Kendall sat beside Scottie. Catching my eye, the doctor shook his head. We'd arrived at the canyon too late. The old man had died.

There was no doubt in my mind that the caretaker had been killed because of something he witnessed at the mission the day Hank died. It seemed most unlikely that, elderly and arthritic, he had made his way to that remote spot above the canyon on his own and accidentally fallen to his death. I was certain an autopsy would show something more than a heart attack. But why was he killed? Had he witnessed the fatal struggle at the top of the tower? If so, why hadn't he spoken up when the sheriff questioned him? Had someone threatened him? Or had the old boy been blackmailing the killer?

Once again my mind returned to that day at the mission when Charles Bragg had appeared out of the blue to rescue me from the dogs. What was he doing there at that particular moment? Had he just killed Hank? If so, why? He had made no secret of his animosity towards the Dorsett family. Did that animosity extend to their farm manager?

But when I expressed my suspicions to Evie a little later back at the cottage, she was as adamant in Charles's defense as I had been in Buck's earlier.

"Nonsense," she said, placing a cigarette in the elegant ebony holder. She had apparently decided on total defiance of Buck and his no-smoking rules. "And I don't know why you keep harping on it.

Granted Charles has a blind spot where poor Hilda's concerned, but there's no way you can convince me that charming man could be so evil. No, my dear. I think that blow on the head has made you delusional. You had better take George Kendall's advice and go to the hospital for a check-up. And get them to x-ray that hip while you're at it."

Though I had hit my head in the fall, it was my hip that bothered me most. I had landed heavily on the hard ground. Already a lump was forming. It would probably be weeks before it went down.

I thought it prudent to change the subject, and told her of another concern.

Something that had been nagging at the back of my mind for days had been brought to the fore with Scottie's death: I was worried about his dogs. Earlier I had merely been trying to figure out how to go about getting them altered, but now a bigger problem had arisen. What was to become of them now that their lord and master was gone? They were hardly prime candidates for adoption.

Evie's reaction was not surprising. "Really, my dear, with everything else that's going on, I don't know how you can bother yourself with a pack of mongrels. Must you be so exhaustingly earnest about every animal that crosses your path?"

"But we can't leave them there to starve," I protested.

"No-one's suggesting we do," she said, humouring me. "I'm sure one of the ranch hands can take care of them perfectly well." She smiled at me indulgently. "You know, sweetie, it's all very well to be concerned about animals, but it doesn't do to appear eccentric."

"Eccentric?" I said, alarmed at the thought. "Whatever do you mean?"

"How about the day we were supposed to be out on a nice shopping spree and you practically accosted a woman in a pet shop for not getting her dog spayed?"

"She jolly well deserved it. It was a mutt, and she'd brought in a litter of its puppies to sell," I protested. "Who knows how carefully she checked the homes for them?"

Evie blew a smoke ring and watched it rise before replying. "I'm sure you're right," she placated. "All I'm saying is that some people might think you're a bit peculiar, the way you harp on things."

That was the second time she'd accused me of harping that afternoon. But she was spared any further outburst from me by a slight commotion coming from the kitchen. "Ah. Here's Tony with the tea." She sounded relieved.

Tony handed me a cup, though most of the tea was in the saucer by the time he'd navigated his way between Trixie and Watson, who were dancing attendance on the biscuit tin in his other hand.

After a couple of sips I put my feet up on the couch and rested my head against the pillow Evie had thoughtfully placed there for me. It was all too much. I could feel my mind giving way. I closed my eyes, only to open them after what seemed like a mere minute or two when I heard a knock on the door, then Mallory's voice.

"How are you feeling? I hear you took a bad fall," he said.

He looked particularly nice, comforting even, in jeans and sports jacket, his shirt open at the neck. Too bad this wasn't a social call.

I pulled myself together. "Better, thank you."

"Good." He took a seat near the couch. "Are you up to answering a few questions?"

"I think I can manage." I smiled.

Tony and Evie seemed suddenly to find a need to be elsewhere. "Well I'll leave you to it," said Evie. "I'm going to call the hospital and see if they can fit you in this afternoon." She turned to Mallory. "Don't stay too long. She needs to rest."

Mallory nodded, then turned a hard stare in Tony's direction.

Tony gathered up the tea things. "And I'll get back to the kitchen," he said. "Then I think I'll take the dogs for a walk."

At his "Walkies, anyone?" both Watson and Trixie jumped up and began running circles around him again. Chamois bounced tentatively on the outskirts.

Mallory's eyes followed Tony out of the room, then turned to me. There was genuine concern in his voice when he said, "I'm sorry that my suggestion you go on the trail ride turned out so badly."

I shrugged. "You know me well enough to know that if I hadn't wanted to go I wouldn't have. I had my own reasons. I wanted to see the wild horses. Besides, if I hadn't gone, and taken a fall just there, it might have been weeks before Scottie was found."

He nodded. "Yes. I suppose we have you to thank for that." He took out his notebook. "Were you able to get anything useful out of Tully?"

"No. I don't know what you think you have on him, but he swears he hasn't been near the mission in weeks. The day of the murder he says he went into L.A. for supplies, and was gone most of the day. That should be easy enough to check."

Mallory looked at his notes. "What if I told you I have an eye witness who saw him in the vicinity of the caretaker's cottage around the time of the murder?"

I shifted my weight off my hip. It was being most troublesome. "I'd say that someone is lying, and my instincts tell me that it's not Austin Tully. I really think you should take another look at Charles Bragg. I told you I saw him at the mission that day. Isn't it possible that the caretaker saw something incriminating and threatened to go to the police? And was killed because of it?"

I paused for breath and Mallory interrupted. "Your powers of deduction never cease to amaze me. If jumping to conclusions was an Olympic event, you'd have a gold medal. Where's the evidence? You've reached this conclusion before the coroner has even established the cause of death. An old man like that, he could have fallen after a heart attack."

He had a way of mocking me which I found quite exasperating.

"Scoff all you like," I said. "What was he doing way out there then? Next you're going to say he fell while rappelling down the canyon."

He overlooked my sarcasm. "You're forgetting one thing. The caretaker wasn't the only one to see Charles Bragg at the mission that afternoon. You were there, too. If we are to follow your line of argument to its ridiculous conclusion, we could assume that you are at risk of being Bragg's next victim."

I must say that particular angle hadn't occurred to me, but after conceding that he had a point, I said, "Which makes it all the more likely that Scottie was not only on the scene, but actually witnessed the murder."

"In which case, why didn't he say something when Anna questioned him?"

"Maybe he was too scared."

Mallory asked me a few more questions about the circumstances of my fall, and the discovery of the caretaker, finishing with, "You pretty much corroborate what the other riders have said, so," he pocketed his notebook with a deliberation which told me he had something else on his mind, "I don't think we need to keep you here any longer," he finished.

I gave him a look of inquiry, and he continued, "The investigation into the horse's death is now part of our official inquiry, and as Mrs. Dorsett-Bragg has already said that she no longer needs your services, you are free to return to Surf City as soon as you like. As for your suspicions about Bragg, I'll keep them in mind."

Another rebuff. Until that moment I'd been looking forward to leaving for home as soon as I felt up to the drive. The following day, if possible. But to be dismissed! While my common sense told me he was merely extending a courtesy, I couldn't help feeling that he was trying to get rid of me.

I had difficulty keeping the disappointment out of my voice. "I'll decide if and when I want to leave, thank you very much," I said. I thought at the very least he would have thanked me for helping with Tully. Not to mention bringing my suspicions about Charles Bragg to his attention. After all, I was now the only one who'd seen Charles at the mission that day, and who had observed that there was some association between him and the caretaker.

Evie came back into the room with Tony and the dogs in tow. "I've made you an appointment for four o'clock," she said. "I'm sorry I shan't be able to take you, but I must stay and help Hilda. She's taking this latest tragedy very hard. An old family retainer gone. Another funeral to arrange. It's really very trying to have people dropping dead all over the place. But Tony, the dear boy, has offered to go with you. I don't want you driving yourself in your condition."

It was on the tip of my tongue to ask her what condition that might be. I felt perfectly capable of driving myself the short distance to the hospital. I only agreed because I knew that further argument would be futile, with Mallory and Tony certain to align themselves with her.

I looked at Watson, sitting patiently by my side. It would be too warm to leave her in the car, and once inside the hospital, who knew how long I might be.

Evie saw my hesitation. "Not to worry," she said. "I'll look after Watson." She smiled at Tony, a favourite of hers. "And little Trixie, too," she said. "If she promises to be good."

Tony grinned. "When is she anything else?"

"Oh please, dear boy. We don't have time to go into that."

Mallory took his leave, nodding to Tony and Evie, and saying to me, "I'll see you back in Surf City, then?" The obvious implication being that he didn't want to set eyes on me again before then.

I smiled and bit my tongue on the retort that I now had absolutely no intention of returning home until the mystery had been solved.

CHAPTER 21

The Game's Afoot

Doris waved us down as we were pulling out of the driveway in Tony's woody and asked if we'd mind giving Lucy a lift to the hospital for her appointment with her obstetrician.

"Robert usually takes her, but he's nowhere to be found, and I don't like her driving herself now her due date's so close." She looked harried. "I'd take her myself, but there's so much to do here, with new guests arriving, and Hilda busy arranging Scottie's funeral."

Tony backed up the wagon to the front porch where Lucy stood waiting in the shade, and she waddled out to the car. I offered her the front seat, thinking she'd be more comfortable, but she preferred to sit in the back.

We drove along tree-lined country roads nearly empty of traffic and uncluttered by commercial development to Dorsetton, about five miles from the ranch. Founded, as much else in those parts, by Hilda's grandfather, it turned out to be hardly more than a rustic mountain village, sleepy in the late afternoon sunshine. The main street retained its original false-front stores, wooden sidewalks, and hitching rails. A lone red stop light blinked aimlessly at the one intersection.

The community hospital reminded me of the cottage hospitals

back in England. Large clay pots of red geraniums lined the driveway dividing broad expanses of lawn, where water sprinklers made rainbows for darting sparrows and finches. Pink and blue hydrangeas bordered the white stucco one-storey building. The parking lot was almost empty, a single ambulance at the end of the driveway the only indication that this was a place where emergencies could occur. It was no surprise that Evie had been able to get me in at short notice.

Lucy's appointment was for four-thirty, a half hour later than mine, so she and Tony decided to walk across the street to the ice cream parlour while I went in for my X-ray.

A well-fed black-and-white cat dozed in the entry way. He eyed me lazily but made no effort to move. I stepped around him into the lobby.

The receptionist, a young woman in her twenties, looked up from her paperback romance novel.

"You must be Mrs. Doolittle. I hear you took a nasty fall this morning out at Wild Horse Canyon."

I smiled. "News travels fast."

She gave me some forms on a clipboard. "My husband's the ambulance driver. He brought in Scottie's body."

I barely had time to fill in name, address, social security number, insurance company (none), and next of kin (Evie, for all intents and purposes), when the radiologist's nurse appeared to usher me into the lab. My hip was x-rayed from every possible angle, and I was instructed that Dr. Kendall would be notified of the results within twenty-four hours. I paid the bill with plastic and was back in the parking lot in less than thirty minutes. Tony and Lucy were leaning against the wagon licking their ice cream cones.

"That looks delicious," I said, eyeing Tony's chocolate cone.

"'ome-made," said Tony. "Can't be beat. If we'd known you was going to be so quick, we'd have got you one."

"Here, you can finish mine," said Lucy, handing me her cone. "I'd better get going. Don't know how long it's going to take. Last time the doctor wasn't here and I just had lab tests. They said to allow more time today, so it might take a while."

She seemed apprehensive, and I wondered what could have kept Robert, who appeared to have no gainful employment, from this important appointment with his wife.

"Would you like me to come in with you?" I offered.

"No, that's okay. Just wait in the car, like Robert always does. He never comes in. He's deathly afraid of hospitals."

I dropped the dripping cone in a nearby dustbin, and watched as she entered the building.

"That's funny," I said to Tony.

"What? Funny ha-ha or funny peculiar?"

"Peculiar. I distinctly remember Mallory telling me Offley had confirmed Robert's alibi that he was at the hospital with Lucy the day Hank Carpenter was killed."

Tony got back in the car, leaving the door open so he could stretch out his leg. He had dispensed with Hilda's cane but the leg was still stiff. "What's your point?" he said.

I eased into the passenger seat. My hip ached. "If Robert waited in the car—didn't go in with Lucy—then who confirmed his alibi? Who was the eye witness that corroborated Lucy's statement that Robert brought her to the doctor's that day?"

"Probably the receptionist, or the doctor."

"Not the doctor. Lucy just said that the last time she was here she only had lab tests."

"Maybe it was the lab technician?"

"Or maybe Lucy's lying. And the only reason she'd lie about such a thing would be because…?"

Tony finished my sentence: "…she's covering for her old man."

"Let's not jump to conclusions. I've already been warned about that once today," I said. "Maybe the receptionist did actually see Robert that day, somehow, and told the cops so." I opened the car door. "Hang on a tick. I'll be right back."

" 'ere, where you off to?"

But by then I was halfway across the parking lot, and just waved back at him.

The receptionist, her head once more in her book, looked up when she heard the door open. "Hi. Forget something?"

"No. I'm waiting for Lucy Dorsett-Bragg. We gave her a lift. Her husband Robert usually brings her, but he was busy today, and couldn't make it. Do you know them well? Robert and Lucy?"

"I see Lucy every week. But Robert always waits in the car. She says he doesn't like hospitals. Afraid he might catch something, I guess." She laughed.

"So you didn't actually see him when he brought Lucy last week, then?"

"No. Like I said. He never comes in."

"You didn't go outside and see him?" I persisted.

Her expression told me she thought it an odd question.

"Well, now that you mention it. I went outside for a cigarette." She gave an embarrassed laugh. "I know. I ought to know better. Like I told that policeman, Sergeant Offal, or something…"

"Sergeant Offley," I corrected.

"Whatever. I told him I saw their car. The red Corvette."

I felt I'd pressed her far enough, but had to make one last attempt. It was important. "And you actually saw Robert?"

"No. Come to think of it, I didn't. I just saw the car, and I guess I assumed he was in it." She raised her palms in a defensive gesture. "He's been bringing Lucy for weeks now."

"But you told the sergeant you saw him?"

She looked confused. "I guess I did. I *thought* I saw him. Why? Is it important?" She sounded defensive. "We were busy that day. There'd been an accident. A truck went off the road. I'd only just lit up when I got called back in."

She turned to some paperwork on her desk, indicating that she had no more to say on the subject. So, with a "Well, I mustn't keep you from your work. Nice chatting with you," I made my way back to the car to report to Tony.

"It's clear that whatever she actually saw, she left Offley with the impression that she had seen Robert."

Tony listened with interest. "You were right then. Lucy's covering for Robert." He scratched his head. "What do you make of it?"

"How about this scenario? Hank found out that Robert killed the horse, and told him he was going to tell Hilda. So Robert killed Hank."

"And why did Robert kill the horse?"

"To get his hands on the insurance money? Maybe he'd been helping himself from the till." My brain was working overtime. "Then Robert planted the evidence of Hank's mismanagement to make it look like he'd have good reason to kill the horse for the insurance money. When he learned Hank was going to see about repairing the bell tower that day, he seized the opportunity, got there ahead of him, lay in wait, and shoved him off the tower."

Tony broke in. "It was Lucy's day for her doctor's appointment, and he got her to cover for him." He shook his head. "I don't know. Doesn't sound like Lucy."

"My guess is, she doesn't know the real reason he didn't take her," I said.

Tony looked doubtful. "What is it?" I asked.

"The receptionist says she saw the Corvette. Would he let Lucy drive it?"

"Probably not, as a rule. But this was an exceptional situation."

"Then how did he get to the mission?"

"There's a couple of ranch pickups he could use. More likely he'd walk. Less conspicuous. It would take fifteen or twenty minutes through the woods, but he'd be able to stay out of sight."

Tony agreed that walking was Robert's most likely option. "One other thing," he said. "He don't strike me as being a particularly bright spark. He'd have needed help to pull off a stunt like that. Cook the books, I mean."

I nodded. "Someone familiar with the the farm's business. Maybe the accountant."

I told him of my encounter with Hicks the day after I arrived. "Robert was there, in Hicks's office. They'd been arguing. Quite heatedly. Robert nearly knocked me over when he stalked out in a huff. Trixie barged in chasing a cat, and I got chatting with Hicks." I smiled, recalling the turmoil Trixie created. "I was surprised he confided so much of the company's business to me, a perfect stranger."

"Maybe he twigged you was an investigator of some sort, and wanted to put you off the scent."

I let the "of some sort" slide. "I wondered about that, and asked Evie if anyone could have overheard her talking to Hilda about me. She said she thought Austin Tully, the vet, might have. Mallory's still working on his alibi."

"Maybe the vet passed on the info to the accountant, in all innocence, like."

"That could be."

"Did you ever find out why they were arguing?" asked Tony.

"Seymour said it was over an unpaid bet he was supposed to have put down for Robert."

A knowing look crossed Tony's face. "Gambling, eh? What's he look like, this Hicks bloke?"

"Tall. Thinning blond hair. Fortyish. Bland face, except for a small scar on his chin. Flashy dress—"

Tony interrupted me with a look of surprise. " 'ang on. *That's* Seymour Hicks? Why didn't you say so before? I bet it's the same bloke as goes by the monicker Sandy Hickock. I know him from the old days. In the nick for embezzlement that time, he was. That's where he got that scar. Nasty bit of work. Dab 'and with the numbers, though." His look turned serious. "I'm warning you, luv, if you're dealing with the likes of 'im, you'd better let the old Bill 'andle it."

Though the days when he had engaged in such pastimes as breaking and entering and other petty crimes were, he claimed, long past, Tony managed to keep remarkably well informed on the doings of the underworld, and maintained an intriguing network of malefactors and malcontents. So I wasn't really surprised by this latest display of inside information.

Ignoring his remark about the police for the moment, I continued with my likely scenario. "Okay. So, Hicks and Robert were cooking the books. One of them, probably Robert, killed Hank Carpenter."

"You're right there," Tony put in. "Old Sandy Hickock, he'd be too smart to dirty his hands with murder."

I gasped. "Then Robert killed Scottie because he saw him push Hank off the tower."

"But why didn't the old geezer tell the police what he'd seen?" asked Tony.

"Perhaps loyalty to the family kept Scottie quiet, but Robert couldn't be sure he could trust him. Or maybe," I voiced the thought that had occurred earlier, "Scottie was blackmailing Robert."

Tony ran a gnarled thumb around his chin. "You'll have to tell Mallory. 'Specially now that we can guess it's Sandy Hickock what's mixed up in it."

"After the way Mallory spoke to me today when I tried to put the blame on poor Charles Bragg," I blushed at the thought, "I'm not telling him anything else unless I have proof."

"What proof? And where are you going to get it?"

"I don't know. But if it's blackmail, then a good place to start looking is Scottie's cottage." I looked at him. "Are you in?"

"Try and keep me out," said my partner in crime. "Someone's got to keep an eye on you."

He looked over toward the hospital. "Watch out. Here she comes. Talk later."

CHAPTER 22

The Caper

Watson left me in no doubt she didn't approve of my going out late at night without her. I tried to slip out before she noticed, but she roused from what I thought was a deep slumber, shook, and prepared for walkies, nosing at her leash and wagging her tail in anticipation. I would have taken her with me, but I couldn't risk another set-to with Scottie's mangy beasties.

"Shh. Be a good girl," I said. "I shan't be long."

Evie, on the other hand, was blissfully unaware of my clandestine escapade. She'd obliged by going to bed with a sleeping pill and black satin eye mask immediately after dinner, having declared herself "completely done in by this entire business."

Tony drove past the mission and parked off the road behind a stand of trees about three hundred yards further on.

A full moon threw everything into deep contrast, and where the cottage had appeared merely neglected by day, by moonlight it looked downright sinister. Beyond the silent graveyard the bell tower loomed black against the clear night sky, the crumbled crenellated walls giving mute testimony to what had occurred there.

Though we had no clear strategy, our immediate concern was the dogs. We hoped to take them by surprise, giving us a better chance to get them under control. But first we had to locate them.

I'd been worrying about those wretched hounds ever since discovering Scottie's body, wondering what would eventually happen to them.

At dinner Austin Tully had told me that, after the trail ride, he'd ridden over to the cottage to put out fresh food and water for the dogs. "When things calm down I'll see what I can do about finding homes for them," he reassured me. "Individually they might turn out to be passable pets. I'll probably keep one myself."

At my expression of surprise that he considered the unruly animals to be adoptable, he said, "They're not as fierce as they look. They just need training. Truly a case of their bark being worse than their bite. It's just that they've never been socialised. Old Scottie was a loner, and the dogs aren't used to strangers. I'll ask around. Maybe one of the local ranchers would be willing to take them on. There's a herding strain in their background that might be developed."

He smiled, anticipating my next question. "And yes, I'll see that they're fixed before I place them."

That was all well and good, but tonight Tony and I still had a pack of unpredictable animals to deal with. Nevertheless, they had provided us with the excuse we needed should we be unfortunate enough to run afoul of the law.

"Always be ready with a good reason for being anywhere you're not supposed to be," advised Tony. "It may not hold up in court, but it gives you time to get your story straight."

Following his advice I had taken the precaution of bringing along some of my home-made dog biscuits.

"What d'you think you're going to do with them, then?" asked my partner in crime.

"What would you suggest, clever clogs? We have to have something to win the dogs over."

"A couple of pork chops would be more like it."

"Pork chops not being an option, these will have to do."

We ducked under the yellow tape surrounding the cottage. "Do you think there's a chance Mallory or the sheriff are still here?" I said.

"Nah. There's not much they can do in the dark."

We found the dogs corralled in a cement and chain link run in back of the cottage. Naturally, they started to bark as we approached, first one, then another, until they were all carrying on fit to waken the dead in the nearby graveyard. Fortunately, there were no other residences nearby, so the noise was more of a distraction for us than likely to attract the attention of others.

The dogs quietened down once they caught a whiff of the biscuits, though to judge by the way they wolfed them down, it was unlikely that they actually tasted, much less appreciated, the healthful ingredients.

I tucked the last few biscuits back in my pocket in case we needed them on the way out, and we proceeded to the next phase of our operation.

The unlocked back door creaked noisily as we entered the cottage. We didn't want to risk turning on the light, but Tony's torch revealed a sparsely furnished kitchen. Scottie had taken his meals at the big house, and apparently did little, if any, cooking at home. A half-empty bag of store-brand dog kibble stood in one corner, a small, chipped enamel saucepan stuck in the top.

The bedroom was equally spartan. A narrow bed, a moth-eaten easy chair, and a mottled cheval mirror were the only furnishings. The closet contained a well-worn sheepskin jacket, and a couple of flannel shirts on wire hangers. Threadbare jeans and a pair of Wellington boots lay in a pile on the floor.

All gave mute testimony to the frugal, and probably lonely, life of the old man who'd lived there.

The small living room was slightly better furnished. A scarred leather couch, which had probably known better days at the big house, stood against one wall, an end table and a clock radio alongside. On the opposite wall was a two-drawer chest. A three-legged stool stood in a corner near the door.

"What's this then? Some kind of cosh?" asked Tony, picking up a thick, heavy stick from beside the couch.

"It's a shillelagh," I said. "My dad used to have one. He brought it back from a holiday in Ireland. I've been told Scottie never went anywhere without it."

"He didn't 'ave it with 'im when he needed it most, out at the canyon, did he?"

"You're right," I said. "And that proves what I've been trying to tell Mallory. That his death wasn't an accident. In that case the shillelagh would have been found with him. He must have been brutally attacked, taken out to the canyon, and left for dead."

Tony put the club back by the couch and we turned our attention to the chest-of-drawers. He held the torch while I investigated. The top drawer contained a selection of small tools, a bottle opener, a screwdriver, a pencil stub, and a silver penknife with a faded enamel picture of Edinburgh Castle.

The second drawer was stuck and took some jiggling before it finally came out with a start, spilling the contents onto the floor.

"Here we go," said Tony, easing out his stiff leg and bending down to help pick up the papers.

"It'll take all night to go through this lot," I said.

"What are we looking for?"

"Blackmail evidence."

"Like what?"

"I don't know. I'll know it when I see it." I sifted through years of bills, airletters postmarked Glasgow, Christmas cards from years past, and other mementoes.

Tony was getting impatient. "You going to read through every one of them there bits and bobs then?" he said.

"If I have to. What's the point of coming if we're not thorough?" I looked up, exasperated. "Hold the torch still, will you? I can't read with you waving it about like that."

I smoothed out a piece of yellowed newsprint. "Look here. What do you make of this?"

Headlined RANCHER'S DEATH RULED ACCIDENTAL, it was dated some twenty years earlier.

> At an inquest yesterday the death of Daniel Bragg, wealthy horse breeder of Dorsett Valley, was ruled accidental. According to testimony from witnesses Hilda Dorsett-Bragg, the victim's wife, and their employee Donald (Scottie) McDonald, Joseph Dorsett arrived home from a hunting trip to find his son-in-law, Daniel Bragg, beating his wife. During the ensuing struggle Dorsett's gun accidentally discharged, fatally wounding Bragg.
>
> Outside the courthouse, relatives of the dead man protested the verdict, vowing that his death would be avenged. Dorsett, his daughter, and McDonald all refused to comment.

Attached to the clipping with a rusted paperclip was a piece of faded notepaper on which a few lines were scrawled. I was about to read it to Tony when the dogs, silent until that moment, started to bark.

"Shh," said Tony. "Someone's out there."

"It's Robert, come to look for the blackmail evidence," I said in hushed tones. My heart was pounding.

"I'll go take a dekko. You stay put," came the whispered reply.

He was gone before I had a chance to tell him to leave me the torch.

After a moment or two the dogs stopped barking. It was eerily quiet. Then I heard the creak of the kitchen door, and footsteps. Footsteps made by heavy shoes, not Tony's rubber flip-flops. Scared stiff, I looked around for something with which to protect myself. In the light of the moon I caught sight of the shillelagh.

I lifted the three-legged stool closer to the door, climbed up, and as the intruder entered the room, brought the club down hard on his head.

CHAPTER 23

Trouble

The moonlight streaming through the uncurtained window revealed a terrible sight. A man, apparently unconscious, lay in a crumpled heap on the floor.

For one horrible moment I feared I'd killed him, but his language soon proved otherwise.

Sergeant Offley looked up at me with startled eyes. "What the …"

The shillelagh clattered from my hand. "Oh. I say. I am most frightfully sorry."

I jumped down from the stool and was trying to help the burly policeman to his feet when Mallory came in. He turned on the light and surveyed the scene with a look of disbelief.

"Ms. Doolittle. Sergeant. What's going on?"

Offley brushed aside my feeble attempts to assist him and stood up unaided, apparently not as hurt as I'd thought, thank goodness. "Sir," he said, with as much dignity as he could muster, "I found this woman acting in a suspicious manner."

This woman, indeed. He knew perfectly well who I was.

"Nothing suspicious about it," I said. "I conked you on the head with a sh—"

"Then you admit it." Reaching into a rear pocket he pulled out his notebook and began writing.

"Not much use denying it, is there? Caught red-handed, one might say."

Offley turned his hound-dog eyes to Mallory, seeking direction.

Mallory looked at me with a shake of his head. "Go ahead, Sergeant. Do your duty."

Offley cleared his throat and proceeded to inform me that I was under arrest for interfering with an officer of the law in performance of his duty, or words to that effect. Furthermore, let him add—and who was I to stop him?—"for assault on a police officer with a, a—" He pointed a stubby finger to the offending cudgel at his feet. "What is that thing?"

"It's a shillelagh," I leaned towards his notebook. "That's s-h-i-"

"Never mind the spelling," Mallory interrupted impatiently.

"You ought to get it right," I said, "because it's important evidence in Scottie's murder."

"What do you mean?" asked Mallory.

"It belonged to Scottie. Finding it here proves that he didn't go out to Wild Horse Canyon by himself and accidentally fall to his death. He never went anywhere without his shillelagh. Ask anyone at Dorsett Farms. Maybe he was taken to the canyon by force, then so severely beaten that the killer thought he was dead."

I could tell from his expression that Mallory thought I might be on to something.

Offley was still trying to finish his arrest statement. "Then there's breaking and entering."

"What breaking and entering? The door wasn't locked," I said.

Mallory cast me an exasperated look. "What were you doing here anyway?"

"We—" I stopped myself. With Tony's record, it wouldn't do for him to be involved and run the risk of being charged with, for all I knew, a three-strikes felony.

"We?" queried Mallory.

"Me, I said me," I covered. "Me, that is I, was worried about Scottie's dogs, and came by to make sure they had food and water."

"By yourself? In the middle of the night?"

"Evie was sick, and I couldn't get away earlier." I was getting good at this.

"And you expected to find the dogs in the house?"

"I thought I heard a puppy whimpering in here."

Mallory let that slide for the patent lie he must have known it to be.

In the silence that followed Offley put in, "Her accomplice fled the scene, sir."

Just as I was thinking, Good old Tony, looking out for number one, as usual, my erstwhile accomplice poked his head around the door, looked directly at Mallory, and said in the friendliest manner, "Evening, guv." Then, turning to me, "I thought I'd better let you know that them 'ounds 'as got out again." He seemed oblivious of the fact that he was in imminent danger of arrest.

"But how—?" I started to say, but at Tony's warning wink I closed my mouth on the words. It was as if I was catching flies.

Mallory ran his hand through his thick grey hair, a habit that on more pleasant occasions I found rather endearing. "I don't know what you two are doing here, but I doubt if it has anything to do with the dogs. By trespassing on a crime scene you may have allowed the killer to escape."

"I suppose you were expecting the killer to come looking for blackmail evidence," I said.

"That was the general idea," agreed Mallory.

"You want to know what I think?" I asked.

"No. But I'm sure you're going to tell me."

"There's no blackmail evidence to find because that wasn't the motive for killing Scottie."

"Then what was?"

"What we've been saying all along. The killer found out that Scottie had seen him push Hank off the tower, and he killed the old man because he thought he couldn't trust him not to talk. But he was wrong. Scottie would never have revealed the name of the killer."

"What makes you so sure?"

"I'm not at liberty to say."

"Why the hell not?" said Mallory angrily.

Tony and Offley were looking from one to the other of us during this exchange. Tony in amusement, Offley, his fleshy jowls lower than ever, in amazement that someone would speak to his boss so.

"It's a private family matter."

"There is no privacy in a murder investigation."

"It has nothing to do with the case."

"You'll have to let me be the judge of that, Ms. Doolittle. I have to warn you, you'll be in serious trouble if you're withholding evidence."

Tony's look turned from amusement to concern. "Look 'ere, mate," he protested, taking a step toward the detective.

Offley stiffened, ready for action.

"Stay out of this, Tipton," warned Mallory. "We haven't finished with you yet."

Tensions were mounting. I felt I had probably exhausted the limited personal consideration I might expect from Mallory. Since I was ill-disposed to spend the night in jail, I offered up some other evidence, hoping to diffuse the situation.

"I found out something else at the hospital today," I said. "You might find it interesting."

"What is it?" asked Mallory.

"Something that blows Robert Dorsett-Bragg's alibi right out of the water. The receptionist, the one who originally told the sergeant here," I nodded in Offley's direction, "that Robert was at the hospital with his wife the day Hank Carpenter was murdered, told me today that she wasn't at all sure that she did see Robert, since he never goes into the hospital when he takes his wife for her standing appointment. He always waits outside in the car."

I admit to sounding a bit cocky. I could have added that Offley had been derelict in his duty, hadn't pursued the line of inquiry far enough. But one look at the lawmen's faces told me I didn't need to point this out to them. The penny had already dropped.

There was a clatter from the kitchen. I guessed the dogs had found the kibble and knocked the saucepan to the floor. They might make an appearance at any moment. I felt for the biscuits in my pocket.

"So," I asked Mallory. "Am I under arrest, or what?"

"That's up to the sergeant." A nasty red bruise was beginning to show on Offley's forehead. But he waved a hand in a gesture of dismissal.

Just then two of the biggest, meanest-looking members of the dog pack burst into the room.

I threw the remaining biscuits at them, and Tony and I made a quick exit while the attention of dogs and cops alike was otherwise engaged. We knew there would be repercussions, that we hadn't heard the last of this night's escapade, but as Tony had said, we needed time to get our stories straight.

The news-clip was still in my pocket. I didn't consider it germane to the investigation. There was no point in the law getting its grubby mitts on what was a purely personal matter, and one so far in the past that it would do no-one any good at all to reveal.

CHAPTER 24

Revelations

It had been a long, tiring night and I had every intention of sleeping late the next morning. But fate and Jack Mallory had other plans. After only a couple of hours in bed, Evie woke me with the announcement that Detective Mallory and the lovely Anna required everyone ("That's all of us—guests, the family, staff," she said waving her hands dramatically) to meet in the dining room for breakfast at 7.30. "*Tout de* bloody *suite* by the sounds of it, so don't dilly-dally," she commanded.

"I've run your bath, and put out your jeans and a clean shirt. Actually, the shirt's mine. You really should plan better when you go on a trip." She pulled back the covers with a flourish, leaving me feeling chilled and disoriented. "I've already taken Watson for a walk, so hurry, hurry."

Run my bath? Taken Watson for a walk? Despite the constant nagging, Evie really was a brick. She could always be counted on to come through in a pinch.

Nonetheless, she was not about to forgive me for sneaking out last night without telling her, and proceeded to tell me in no uncertain terms how very put out she was. "I don't know where you were last night, or with whom, and on the whole, I think I'd rather not. But whatever you've been up to, you've managed to get your man Mallory in a bit of a lather. Knocked on the door an hour ago, demanding to know where you were. It's a wonder he didn't come in and drag you out of bed himself. I told him to keep a civil tongue and we'd be there for breakfast like good little suspects."

I staggered off to the bathroom mumbling something to the effect that if ever there had been a time when Mallory was "my man," that time had passed, and it was unlikely he would ever speak to me again, except possibly to make an arrest. Evie raised her eyebrows at this, but thankfully kept her resolve to ask no questions. In any case, all would become clear to her soon enough, and if my suspicions were correct as to the reason for the early morning summons, it would be sooner rather than later.

The dining room buzzed with questions: "Why are we here?" "What's up?" "Has there been a breakthrough in the investigation?" When I took my place in line at the breakfast buffet I was surprised that people turned to me for answers. Had my acquaintance with Jack Mallory been more obvious than I'd thought?

"Do you know how long this is going to take?" fussed Marsha Kendall. "It's our last day." The Kendalls' luggage was already stacked in the lobby in readiness for their departure on the shuttle that would be bringing the new contingent of guests from the airport in an hour or so.

She gave me a quick hug. "It's been such a pleasure meeting you," she said, as her husband joined us. "George, I've just been telling Delilah that if she's ever in Chicago she must come visit."

Their two boys had already finished breakfast and asked permission to go and say good-bye to the horses. George looked undecided, and I suggested they ask Detective Mallory, who was standing near the door talking with Offley. He listened to their request and nodded okay. With a quick wave to their mother, the boys left the room.

It turned out that Mallory had already spoken to the staff, including the kitchen help, freeing them to prepare and serve the meal. "I must say, he's been most considerate, trying to create as little disorder as possible," said Doris, stopping by to make sure the serving dishes were full, the plates hot, and the silverware and utensils sufficient.

Robert came in with Lucy hanging on his arm. He stopped to talk to Mallory. "Anything you need," he said pompously, "just say the word."

"It's good to see Robert taking charge," said Evie, stepping in front of me in line and helping herself to fruit salad and a bagel. "Hilda will need to rely on him more than ever now."

Lucy looked pale and tired. Robert should take her to her seat, I thought, instead of throwing his weight around with the police.

I was surprisingly hungry after my night's escapade, and helped myself to a generous plateful of eggs, sausage, fried bread, tomatoes, and hashed brown potatoes, before taking a seat next to Austin Tully and Rusty. They were discussing the health and merits of the Lazy D's large string of trail horses, deciding on the most suitable for the incoming guests on their first trail ride. The young wrangler confided to me that he was sitting by the door ready for a quick getaway as soon as Mallory was finished.

At the far end of the table Buck and Fiona had their heads together. She would soon be returning to England to finish university. They planned to marry the following spring when she came home with her degree. Evie, who had stopped to get tea, eyed them impatiently as she set down her cup, saying that she hoped Fiona would come to her senses in the meantime.

But Hilda, sitting next to Buck, appeared to have reconciled herself to the idea of the young cowboy joining the family. Open in front of her was what looked like a reservation book, and from time to time she would turn to ask something of her intended son-in-law. After a few minutes, she handed the book over to him and turned her attention to the ancient Yorkie sitting in her lap, dipping pieces of toast into her coffee and feeding them to the dog. No wonder he was so cranky. He was over-caffeinated.

There was no sign of Tony. Had he, with his sixth sense for trouble, made his getaway before Mallory's summons came?

Evie gave me a nudge. Following her glance through the window I saw Charles Bragg tying his big white horse (or *grey*, as the Kendall boys had been quick to advise me the day after I arrived) to the hitching rail alongside Buck's horse and the horse-drawn chuckwagon, which was there to pick up provisions for the day's ride.

Hilda's mouth tightened with annoyance when her brother-in-law entered the room. But he seemed not to notice, kissing Lucy and Fiona, and greeting Evie and me most cordially, saying, "I got a message from the sheriff to be here. What's this all about?"

As if on cue Mallory closed the door, walked to the head of the table, and stood beside Hilda. Offley stayed by the door with arms folded. The message was clear: No-one leaves.

The chatter stopped. All eyes were on Mallory.

"I'll try not to keep you any longer than necessary," he said. "Those of you with planes to catch, I promise to get you out of here in good time."

He apologised to Marsha and George Kendall, and the other guests, saying that while none of them were suspects, they might, in some cases, be able to corroborate the sequence of events, or in others, to confirm alibis.

Evie leaned her head close to mine. "That lets us out, sweetie," she murmured. "I knew all that third degree stuff was a waste of time."

Mallory gave her a stern look and continued. "The events leading up to the murders started several weeks ago with the death of one of Mrs. Dorsett-Bragg's champions."

At the mention of her beloved Duke of Paddington Hilda took a lace handkerchief from her sleeve and wiped away an unseen tear.

Mallory patted her shoulder sympathetically, then continued. "For a time it was believed that the horse had been deliberately poisoned, and that the murders were connected in some way. We now know that wasn't the case."

Fiona voiced the question on many lips. "What *did* happen then?"

Mallory turned to Austin. "I'll let Dr. Tully fill you in."

The vet cleared his throat. "We finally received the autopsy report back from a second independent lab, which confirms the first. The Duke died from a ruptured stomach and peritonitis, triggered by the administration of a drug overdose."

At this there was a collective gasp from family members, but before further speculation could begin, Austin continued. "It was, I regret to say, Bute, or phenylbutazone, a painkiller we've routinely given the Duke in the past with no problem. The night before I went to the CVMA conference I observed that he was restless, not himself, so I gave him the medication believing it would hold him until I got back." From under his chair he produced the meds chart he'd shown me that day at the stable. "That dose is clearly marked off. But the lab findings indicate that within twenty-four hours an additional dose was administered." He put down the chart with a sigh. "There was no further dose marked off."

Hilda stood up abruptly, causing little Nifty to jump awkwardly to the floor. "It was me. I went to the stable Saturday evening and thought the Duke was unusually restless." Her voice trembled. "So I gave him another dose of Bute. I forgot to look at the chart first. I killed my own horse."

She sat down, put her head on the table, and sobbed. Fiona left her seat to comfort her mother.

"So that's what happened," said Austin. He looked almost as distressed as his employer. "Mrs. Dorsett-Bragg, I'm truly sorry."

Mallory took up the story again. "The horse's death, which we can now attribute to human error, set in motion a chain of events that eventually resulted in the deaths of two people. At first it appeared that Hank Carpenter had taken his own life, the theory being that he killed the horse in the expectation that a sudden infusion of insurance money would help cover up an embezzlement of farm funds, and that he had subsequently killed himself in a fit of remorse."

"All lies," murmured Doris, who had taken a seat beside Evie. "My husband did not write that note."

"We proved that early on," said Mallory. "The note was typed on Mrs. Dorsett-Bragg's manual typewriter. No secret there. Who by?

That's the question. Plenty of partial fingerprints on the note. Sheriff Banning's, Buck and Mrs. Carpenter's, Ms. Doolittle's."

Evie kicked me under the table. "When will you ever learn?" she whispered.

Mallory raised his eyebrows at her, then went on. "Plenty of prints," he repeated, "including the killer's." He paused for effect. "But not the victim's."

"I told you so!" cried Doris, looking around the room with satisfaction.

I smiled at her, pleased that she finally had proof of her husband's innocence. But Mallory's words echoed in my head. "Prints... including the killer's." Had he already identified the culprit? Then why hadn't he made an arrest? Was he waiting for the killer to make one last move to confirm his suspicion and prove guilt beyond a shadow of a doubt? At that moment I knew that this was more than a simple narration of events. There was yet one more scene to play out. I looked around the room and shuddered. One of these people was a murderer.

Mallory poured himself a glass of water from a carafe on the table, and turned to Hilda. "Who first suggested to you that Hank Carpenter had committed suicide?"

Hilda, not yet recovered from the shocking realisation that she herself was partially responsible for the death of her horse, looked up. "Seymour Hicks, our accountant. And..." Silenced by a warning look from Robert, she looked around the room. "He doesn't seem to be here," she finished lamely.

Mallory nodded. "Carpenter was murdered because he was about to finger the real culprit in the embezzlement. Once his death was proved to be a homicide, the true embezzler had to dispose of the evidence that he'd been siphoning off company funds. The solution? To set fire to the office."

A buzz of surprise greeted this announcement. Evie couldn't resist. She looked at Buck in triumph. "You see. I told you it wasn't my fault."

Buck acknowledged as much by raising his glass of orange juice to her.

Mallory ignored the outburst. "The means to commit the murder was available to anyone capable of pushing the unsuspecting victim off the tower. The motive narrows the field to those who might benefit from Carpenter's death. What remains is opportunity. Which is where the alibis come in."

"Now we're getting somewhere," said Rusty, anxious to get back to his horses.

"We'll start with those whose alibis are watertight," said Mallory. "At the estimated time of death, Mrs. Dorsett-Bragg and Mrs. Carpenter were supervising the staff in meal preparation and housekeeping. More than sufficient witnesses to verify their alibis."

I admired his tact. Doris, for one, may well originally have been a suspect. She wouldn't have been the first woman to kill her husband—nor the last. And Hilda, the beneficiary if the insurance company had paid up, could reasonably have been suspected of killing the farm manager to cover her tracks.

"Miss Fiona Dorsett-Bragg was in the training ring with a student, and was observed there by Ms. Doolittle and Mrs. Cavendish."

"And very pretty she looked, too," said Evie.

"Evie, please do shut up," I whispered.

Mallory took another sip of water. "Buck Carpenter was on the trail ride until mid-afternoon, along with Claude Dombey."

"Who's that?" said Lucy, with a giggle.

"That would be me," said Rusty, his face red with embarrassment.

"That leaves," Mallory glanced at his notes, "Dr. Austin Tully."

Startled, the vet looked up from pouring syrup on his pancakes. He cast a worried look at Mallory while the syrup continued to pour, threatening to swamp the plate.

"Dr. Tully was out of town on business, and his alibi has now been confirmed."

It was with an obvious sigh of relief that Austin returned to his pancakes. (I was to learn later that the reason for his reluctance to be forthcoming with his whereabouts at the time of the murder was that he had been on a scouting expedition in the Santa Barbara area, looking at prospects for re-locating his practice. It seems he'd had it with the Dorsett-Braggs and their problems. Naturally, he had not wanted word of his plans to leak out before he was ready.)

Mallory glanced at his watch. "Only one individual here has no alibi." He turned to Charles, who was at that moment refilling his cup at the coffee urn.

"Charles Bragg has so far been unable to provide us with a verifiable account of his whereabouts. Are you now ready to tell us where you were between the hours of noon and three o'clock that day?"

Charles remained unruffled. "Can't say precisely. As I've told you before, I rode out to Wild Horse Canyon and back. I took my time, and got to the mission at just about the same time as Mrs. Doolittle."

At that moment I happened to glance in Robert's direction. He wore a look of what I can only describe as smug relief. That same expression was reflected in his mother's face.

"You were right after all," Evie whispered to me. "Who'd have thought it was Charles?"

I couldn't share her satisfaction, embarrassed to think I had played a part in leading Mallory to the conclusion Charles was the culprit. The fact that I had since turned my suspicions in Robert's direction, and had told Mallory so, hardly exonerated me.

Fiona looked alarmed at the suggestion her favourite uncle was under suspicion, but said nothing, no doubt prepared, as was I, to wait for Mallory's further revelations on the subject.

Lucy, on the other hand, had become quite agitated. She dropped her cereal spoon with a clatter. "Not Uncle Charlie," she protested.

The silence that greeted this outburst was broken by a knock on the door. Offley stood aside and Sheriff Banning entered, along with two deputies. Almost as if choreographed, the deputies took up positions one each side of Charles. Anna sat down at the table, near Mallory.

"Am I under arrest?" asked Charles. He seemed almost amused. I didn't think he had anything to smile about.

"We're not finished yet," said Mallory. He glanced around the room to make sure he still had everyone's attention. He did. We were all sure he was about to make an arrest. Even Rusty had stopped fidgeting.

"The killer had learned that Scottie McDonald, the mission caretaker, had seen him push Hank Carpenter off the bell tower. It's possible he realised at the time he'd been observed. Or maybe McDonald was blackmailing the killer. We're still investigating that angle. Whatever, in the killer's mind a second murder became necessary to cover up the first. Evidence strongly suggests that McDonald was brutally assaulted in his cottage, then left for dead out at Wild Horse Canyon."

At least I'd got that part right, I thought. But my self-congratulations were short-lived.

"In addition to McDonald's fingerprints, there were three other sets on the murder weapon. One of which," he turned to me with a shake of his head, "belongs to Ms. Doolittle."

The shillelagh. Oh no. To think that I had handled the murder weapon. Tony, too.

"Really, Dee!" declared Evie. "Your fingerprints everywhere! I knew it was a mistake to bring you here."

Charles appeared to be the only one enjoying the joke. "So you're my partner in crime, Mrs. Doolittle," he said.

I could stand it no longer. "But Scottie would never have betrayed the killer. He… Here." I pulled the clipping from my pocket, and casting a look of apology at Hilda, handed it to Mallory.

CHAPTER 25

Showdown

"Where did you find this?" Mallory demanded.

"At Scottie's cottage," I stammered, my face burning, as well it ought.

He quickly scanned the clipping and the attached note, then handed them to Hilda. "They don't have much relevance to the current case, except to reveal a gross miscalculation on the killer's part. So," his tone softened, "you're under no obligation to share them with everyone."

Hilda's hand trembled as she took the yellowing papers. If it hadn't been for Doris and Fiona supporting her, she might have fainted. "No," she said. "It all happened so long ago, there's no point in keeping the secret any longer." Her voice gained strength as she handed the clipping and note back to Mallory. "Go ahead. Read it."

We listened with rapt attention as Mallory read the clipping aloud, then, out of deference to Hilda, I'm sure, indicated that the attached note was from Mrs. Dorsett-Bragg, thanking Scottie for coming to her rescue.

"I don't understand," said Fiona. "What had Scottie to do with Grandfather's shooting my father?"

Hilda reached over and took her daughter's hand. "Scottie saved my life. It was he, not your grandfather, who shot Daniel." Her look pleaded for understanding. "I'm sorry, dear. I've tried to shield you and Robert from the truth all these years. But your father was an abusive man. That night he was drunk and attacked me quite brutally. It wasn't the first time. Each time was worse than the last. Finally I could stand it no longer and told him I intended to file for divorce. He said he would kill me rather than allow that. He left the room and I hoped he was going to sleep it off, but he returned with a gun."

Her voice so low I had to strain to catch her words, Hilda continued to relate the events of that fateful night. "Scottie knew Daniel was on one of his binges, and came to the house to make sure I was all right. If he hadn't arrived when he did, I'm quite sure Daniel would have killed me. They struggled, the gun went off, and Daniel was dead. Just like that. It happened so fast."

She closed her eyes, as if reliving the scene. "At that moment your grandfather came home. He immediately grasped what had happened, and insisted on taking the blame himself rather than risk Scottie's being tried for murder. He wiped Scottie's fingerprints from the gun, leaving his own. Your grandfather knew the authorities were more likely to go easy on a rich, influential landowner claiming an accident, than on a ranch hand who some," she cast a quick look in Charles's direction, "might have accused of a crime of passion."

At Fiona's expression of surprise at the hint of an indiscretion, Hilda added hastily, "Not that there was anything like that. No. But Scottie," she hesitated, then said, "well, there was no question that he was devoted to me."

"But why would your father take such a risk?" asked George Kendall. "There was no way he could be sure of an accidental death verdict."

"You have to understand the ties that bound those two," said Hilda. "They had started out as young boys together back in England. They came to California with the dream of building a horse farm together. Though Scottie lacked my father's drive and ambition, Father told me many times that the farm's success was due to Scottie's almost intuitive understanding of breeding. Father truly believed he would never have accomplished what he did without his childhood friend by his side. Unfortunately, though they shared equally in the rewards of their efforts, Scottie made some unwise business decisions of his own, and finally he was reduced to living in the mission cottage. More than that he was too proud to accept from us."

It was becoming clearer. The killer's secret was safe with Scottie because the caretaker owed a moral debt to the killer's family. But which family? The Dorsetts, out of loyalty and gratitude? Or the Braggs, his silence born of guilt for having killed Charles's older brother?

Hilda turned to Charles. "I'm sorry. But you had to know sooner or later. I've tried to tell you many times over the years, but there was so much ill-feeling between us. Understandably, since you never knew the truth. You were just a child at the time."

I observed Charles closely for his reaction to having heard his brother described as a thoroughly bad lot. It was a great deal for a man to process after carrying a grudge against the Dorsetts his entire life. His expression turned from confusion to acceptance, almost as if something clicked in his memory and finally made sense. I wondered if Scottie had ever attempted to tell Charles the truth. Certainly I now understood why he had been reluctant to accept Charles's offers of help.

The tension created by Hilda's dramatic recital of long-ago events was broken by the shuffling of chairs and the murmur of voices as people looked at their watches.

Mallory sensed their impatience. "I won't keep you much longer." He craned his neck to see out the window. "The bus isn't here yet." He took a sip from his glass. "We've established that the reason Carpenter was killed was most likely because he suspected that someone was embezzling farm funds, and perhaps he was preparing to go to Mrs. Dorsett-Bragg with the information. This means that the killer was someone with easy access to the accounts, or who had an accomplice who was."

"And how am I supposed to benefit from any of this?" asked

Charles. The deputies remained standing on either side of him, giving very much the appearance that he was under guard. "I have no access to Dorsett Farms accounts, and the insurance money sure as hell wouldn't be coming my way."

"A motive has yet to be discovered," replied Mallory, "but you definitely had the opportunity. And we did have two witnesses who could place you at the scene at the time Carpenter was killed." He paused. "One of them is now dead."

I gave an involuntary shudder. I was the other witness.

"Circumstantial," scoffed Charles. "You'll have to do better than that."

Brave words. But from where I sat it appeared that the net was closing in on Charles.

Lucy, too, seemed to realise the import of Mallory's words. Wide-eyed, she turned from one to the other. "Not Uncle Charlie," she cried again.

Buck, who had been following Mallory's words closely, now said, "Where's Seymour?"

I'd been so busy paying attention to the rest of the goings-on that I hadn't noticed that the accountant hadn't shown up for breakfast.

"Scarpered," said an unmistakable Cockney voice from the doorway. "Done a bunk. I saw him leave late last night."

A look passed between Mallory and Sheriff Banning. She nodded. "We caught up with him," she said. "He was picked up at the overseas terminal at LAX early this morning."

I realised that Mallory had been busy long after Tony and I had left Scottie's cottage the previous night.

Tony slipped into the seat next to Evie.

"Where have you been, dear boy?" she asked.

"I had a bit of business to take care of," he said. He leaned behind Evie and gave me a wink, which I interpreted as meaning he'd had something to do with either the accountant's apprehension or attempted escape. With Tony one was never quite sure on which side of the law he might land.

Robert meanwhile, was on his feet. "Gone! He can't be gone. He said he…"

Mallory and Anna were listening intently, but Robert hesitated a moment, then appeared to alter course. "Did he have the money with him?" he asked the sheriff.

"What money?" queried Mallory.

Robert looked confused. "This morning I discovered some cash missing from the floor-safe in the office. Or what's left of the office after the fire," he covered. I knew he was lying. His face was flushed and he avoided looking Mallory in the eye.

My mind went back to that first day at the stable when I'd overheard Robert warning Seymour to keep his mouth shut. At the time I had believed Seymour's explanation that Robert's outburst had something to do with a bet gone bad. Now I realised it was more likely that Robert had wanted Seymour to give him an alibi for the time of Carpenter's death.

Lucy must have come to a similar conclusion. "You told me you were at the track," she accused her husband.

"What are you talking about? Don't you feel well?" he said, suddenly solicitous of her health. "Let me take you home," he added in what was clearly a blatant attempt to escape the uncomfortable position in which he suddenly found himself.

But the enormity of what he had done was dawning on her. "The day Hank was killed, that was the day I went to the hospital by myself. But you told me to say that you came with me, because you were at the track and you didn't want your mother to find out."

There was a gasp from Hilda. How many more shocks was the poor woman to endure?

"You're confused," Robert told his wife. "That was the previous week."

"No. It was just last week," she insisted. She turned to Charles. "I'm so sorry. I didn't know it would get you into trouble."

Charles took a step forward as if to comfort her, but the deputies closed in.

I opened my mouth to say something about being able to confirm what Lucy had said. But a glance at Mallory showed me he had everything under control. I realised that he had manipulated the entire scene, had known the script before we had even assembled for breakfast. Like a film director, he knew in advance how each player would react. Me, Hilda, Charles, Robert, and particularly, poor Lucy. He'd known about Robert's bogus alibi, thanks to me, but he wanted Lucy to expose him and admit to her part in the cover-up. I wasn't sure I approved of his methods. But he got results, and that was his job.

By now Robert must have realised that he'd made too many mistakes. My guess was that Seymour had been the brains of the doomed enterprise. Now he'd tried to flee, and probably at that very moment was conferring with his attorney, preparing to implicate Robert in the hopes of a plea bargain.

"Seymour's the one you want. He killed Carpenter, and now he's taken off, and left me holding the bag," Robert blurted out.

Hilda was obviously having trouble taking it all in. She took a step towards her son, perhaps to calm him, perhaps to keep him from incriminating himself further. But Robert brushed her aside, snatched the cane from her hand, and threatened anyone who came near him. "Stay back," he yelled, waving the stick wildly.

Fiona was on her feet. "Robert! Calm down. Have you lost your mind?" she shouted at her brother.

Buck took a chance, ducked under the cane, swung at Robert and missed. The cane came down sharply on his arm, and he backed off.

Leaving the door unguarded, Sergeant Offley stepped forward, made a grab for Robert, and was rewarded with a jagged cut across the face from the silver horse's head.

There was a crash of glass behind me and I turned to see Robert snatch a revolver from the gun case. The next thing I knew, he had grabbed me around the neck and was backing towards the unguarded door.

By this time the lawmen had drawn their weapons but were unable to fire. There was a dozen or more people between them and the lunatic with a gun. Not to mention a hostage; that would be me.

Robert dragged me out the door, down the hall and outside to the driveway where the horses were tethered. Looking around wildly for a means of escape, he forced me aboard the chuckwagon and leaped up beside me. I wanted to struggle free, but I have to admit to a healthy respect for the weapon he carried. Though I guessed that it was unlikely a gun from a display case would be loaded, it wasn't a guess on which I was prepared to risk my life.

Just at that moment the noisy diesel shuttle bus sputtered up the driveway bringing new guests from the airport. Startled as much by the bus as by the commotion aboard their own conveyance, the chuckwagon team bolted.

CHAPTER 26

Hullabaloo

As the terrified horses galloped uncontrolled down the driveway, I was only vaguely aware of the hue and cry behind us. Two imminent dangers loomed: I was either about to be shot by a madman or thrown from the wagon.

Out onto the highway we hurtled on two wheels, the horses swerving left with such fury that our ill-advised outing almost ended right then and there. I was soon regretting the large breakfast I'd just put away.

Robert, his red-faced anger replaced by chalk-white panic, clearly had no idea how to control the team. The reins lay uselessly on the floor, while he clung white-knuckled to the seat with one hand, keeping the revolver trained on me with the other. At the pace we were going his aim couldn't be accurate, but the gun might go off accidentally and still find its mark—me.

Clinging with both hands to the side farthest from my abductor, I watched for an opportunity to jump, but we were going at such a clip I was afraid of being run over by an oncoming car, or not getting clear of the wagon. Besides, there was that gun.

"Can't you stop them?" I shouted over the noise. Pots and pans swung perilously. Their clanging, joined in ominous chorus with rumbling wheels and thudding hooves, drowned out my protests.

Robert appeared not to hear me; his mind no doubt was a jumble of escape plans, recriminations, and the sheer necessity of survival.

We were now galloping across an open field, and after a few bone-jarring jolts over uneven ruts, I saw we were headed for Wild Horse Canyon, the scene of my earlier mishap. Curly's words that day came back to me. *"They don't need a driver. They know exactly where they're headed. Just load up the wagon, point them in the right direction and they'd find their own way, they're so used to the trail. They always get a carrot when they get there."*

Well, there'd be no carrots today.

We came to the top of a steep incline and abruptly began our descent to the canyon floor, gathering more speed as we went. Directly in our path was a low-hanging tree branch. We would have to duck to avoid it. Here was my chance. At the crucial moment I distracted Robert's attention by making a grab for the reins, then ducked as the branch smacked him squarely across the forehead, caught him off balance, and knocked him back inside the wagon.

I picked up the reins and pulled on them—hard—but I was no match for the panicked pair. I realised that somehow I would have to release them. I remembered watching Curly handle the team on the way back from the disastrous trail ride, and desperately tried to recall what I had then observed so casually. I reached along the shaft and unbuckled the harness of the first horse. It galloped off to the right in a cloud of dust. The pace slackened a little, but the weight of the wagon continued to propel us forward.

Releasing the second horse was another matter. The buckles were stiff and it was a one-handed operation. I was holding on for grim life with the other. I also kept a fearful eye on the canvas flap behind me, expecting at any moment to be grabbed from behind by the wild-eyed fugitive. Finally, the harness was loosened, and the second horse veered away from the slowing but still rolling wagon.

Then it was my turn. Judging the distance, I targeted a suitable spot, a large bush that didn't look too prickly, and jumped. The wagon, with Robert, the grub, the dishes, and the pots and pans, rumbled on down the slope to the canyon floor where it crashed.

My hands sore and bleeding from struggling with the harness and from the fall, I got to my knees and stared in horror at the wreckage. The dust was still settling when Buck and Charles rode up.

As Evie told it to me later in an undoubtedly highly coloured account of what happened back at the house after my abduction: "My dear, you simply would not believe the hullabaloo. For a moment or two it was as if everyone was riveted to the spot. But just for a moment." She paused for effect.

"Then everyone started trying to get through the door at the same time. Believe me, the Keystone Kops weren't in it. The young Buck—who I have to admit has improved vastly in my estimation over the past hour or so—and that divine Charles—who, if you gave him half a chance would no doubt make you an offer, and there you'd be, set for life in this rustic environment you seem to thrive on—well, they and that wrangler boy, Rusty, were the first through the door, leaping onto their horses and giving chase like something out of an early western film.

"Your man Mallory and the lovely Anna were hard on their heels, or should one say hooves, in the Jeep. It was all most astonishingly exciting."

Exciting for her, maybe.

"Where's Robert?" Buck now demanded, his handsome young face grim with anger.

"He's still in the wagon. I, I… He was hit rather hard by a tree."

Buck spurred his horse down the slope, while Charles helped me to my feet.

"Never mind about Robert," he said, putting a protective arm around me. "Thank God you're okay."

Embarrassed by his fervour, I squirmed loose and attempted to brush myself down and smooth my hair. "I must look an absolute sketch," I said.

"Mrs. Doolittle," exclaimed Charles, "you look just gorgeous, even after your adventure."

At any other time such astounding dishonesty would have brought forth a tart response, but I was too busy pulling myself together to waste my breath.

Charles had his arm back around me when Mallory, Offley, and Anna drove up in the Jeep. The sheriff remained on the radio while Mallory, after a long stare in our direction had apparently assured him I was still in one piece and in good hands, followed Offley down to the wagon on foot. There they helped Buck pull a badly bruised and shaken Robert from the wreckage. Soon they were coming back up the hill, with Robert's handcuffed hands holding on to Buck's stirrup. None too gently he was hustled into the Jeep, and Mallory, Offley, and the sheriff drove off with him.

Soon afterward Rusty rode up with the errant horses in tow, winded but unharmed, much to my relief. I'd been afraid they might have been hurt after being turned loose so abruptly.

Just as I was beginning to wonder how I was going to get back to the ranch—I didn't much fancy having to ride pillion behind Charles—Tony and Evie arrived in the woody.

"Who d'you think you are, Annie bloody Oakley?" said my fellow countryman.

Evie was more to the point. "Dee, why do you do these things? You've had us all in such a kerfuffle. You never seem to be satisfied unless you have everyone in an uproar." She made it sound as if the entire escapade had been my idea!

"And what were *you* doing while your best friend was in dire jeopardy?" I inquired of her.

"Sweetie, what could I do? I knew that between the law and the cowboys, you couldn't be in better hands." She gave Charles an admiring glance and me a quick hug. "We passed the lovely Anna and her posse on the way here. It looks like it's all over bar the shouting. Mind you," she added, "I always knew there was something a bit off about that Robert. Obviously, he takes after his father—the beastly bloodline, as 'twere."

CHAPTER 27

Sanctuary

Back at the house, we found the family in shock over Robert's treachery and the disgrace he had brought upon the family.

Fiona and Doris had their hands full, trying to comfort Hilda and Lucy. It fell to myself and Evie to cope with the bewildered new arrivals, some of whom were convinced the whole kidnapping episode had been staged for their entertainment, like something out of a western theme park.

Consequently by the time we had provided lunch, escorted the guests to their various cabins, and calmed their concerns about what kind of place they had come to, it was too late in the day for me to consider leaving. I didn't relish negotiating the mountain roads in the dark, and there was really no hurry, as long as I was home in time for Ariel's departure and the promised dog-sitting. Besides, an early start the following day would give me an opportunity to visit the bird sanctuary I had passed on my way in.

I wouldn't be sorry to leave Dorsett Farms and the Lazy D Guest Ranch. The entire enterprise had been a monumental disaster. The death of the Duke of Paddington had been written off as an accident, my retainer barely worth the aggravation, not to mention the medical expenses, whilst the unexpected appearance of Jack Mallory was a complication I could well have done without.

Though she planned to stay on for a few days longer to help Hilda, Evie echoed my sentiments.

"Well, dear. I'm sad to have to say so, but I'll be glad to see the last of this place myself. It's all down to Fiona now. She and her cowboy will have to buckle down and help Hilda run the place. Though, mind you, I intend to do all I can to persuade Hilda to sell. Poor Fiona has had to give up returning to university this year. Much as it dismays me, her place is with her mother."

She was right. Hilda seemed to have aged visibly over the last twenty-four hours.

Evie rustled around in her purse for her cigarettes. Then, no doubt with fire hazards on her mind, she thought better of it and put them away again. "I understand Charles Bragg is interested in buying. Speaking of Charles, it looks like you've let another RNM slip through your fingers. I know he's interested, if you'd just play your cards right. He said he's coming by in the morning to see if you're all right. What a gentleman!"

She gave me a sidelong glance. "I told your detective when he asked after you while you were at the hospital, that you and Charles were becoming quite close."

"Why on earth would you say such a thing?" I demanded.

"Well, I could see how upset you were, with Mallory and the lovely Anna always with their heads together, so I thought I'd fan the flames a little."

Really, there were times when Evie stretched the bonds of friendship to the breaking point.

I hadn't seen Mallory since he left Wild Horse Canyon. No doubt he and Anna would be kept busy wrapping up the case for some time yet.

Tony had already left. He'd helped us make the sandwiches for the dudes' lunch, then announced, "Well, ladies. Me and me dog are off 'ome before anyone else gets done in. I'll see you back in Surf City, Delilah. You won't find me mingling with the 'orsey set again any time soon."

Before he left he'd told us where he'd disappeared to earlier that morning.

"I figured chances were that it was that there shillelagh that was used to do in the old geezer. And, of course, me prints was all over it. So I thought I'd better get that cleared with Mallory first thing. He's a decent enough sort once you get to know him. Any old 'ow, once we got that sorted, he told me they'd checked Seymour Hicks for priors, and like I said, found out he was AKA Sandy Hickock. We figured he'd talked Robert into the scam to help cover Sonny's gambling debts, but the whole deal went sour. And, well, you know the rest."

Indeed I did.

The sign in the sanctuary parking lot said NO DOGS, so I backed up and pulled off the road and parked in the shade of a small grove of trees just outside.

"Shan't be long," I told Watson, cracking the window a few inches for her to put her muzzle out. "I'm just going in for a quick peek. Can't walk too far, anyway, the way my hip's playing me up. But who knows when we'll get the chance again?"

I picked up a trail guide from the box inside the gate, crossed a narrow bridge over a slow-running stream where mallards dozed in the shade of a low-hanging willow, and started down the marked trail. The gentle burble of the water was the only sound to be heard. The birds were silent in the midday sun and I didn't really expect to spot so much as a common sparrow. But it was heaven to have some peace after the turmoil of the last few days.

I was relishing the solitude when I saw to my annoyance that I was not alone. A man was walking on the path ahead of me. I slowed my pace so as not to catch up with him, but rounding a bend in the trail I bumped right into him. He had his field glasses trained on the uppermost branches of an old oak.

"Shh," said Mallory, quickly recovering from his surprise at seeing me.

"I haven't said anything yet," I whispered. I hope he didn't think that I'd followed him. Mind you, I should have guessed he wouldn't pass up the opportunity to visit the sanctuary while he was in the area. "What is it? One of your whatnot boobies?"

He ignored the sarcasm. "I think it's a downy woodpecker." He handed me the glasses and pointed.

There was a rush of wings as a bird flew out of the branches overhead.

"Never mind," he said, annoyed. "You startled it."

"I don't believe it was a downy in the first place," I retorted, consulting the guide. "It's not listed."

High above, a flock of crows, black satiny rags against blue sky, winged their way westward, their harsh cawing muffled by distance. Mallory watched until they passed, then said, "Isn't Charles Bragg with you?"

"Charles? Why would he be? I don't know that he's interested in birds."

"You know what I mean."

"I most certainly don't."

He turned back in the direction of the parking lot. He took long strides and I had to hurry to keep pace with him.

"You seem to have enjoyed flirting with him the past few days."

I would have laughed at his use of the old-fashioned word if I hadn't been so outraged.

"I thought you were too busy solving murders with the lovely Anna"—Evie's phrase slipped out before I could stop it, and he raised his eyebrows in question—"to notice what I was doing. Flirting or otherwise. In fact, I'm surprised you could tear yourself away so soon."

He shrugged. "It's Anna's case. She'll wrap up. I have to get back to my regular job. They'll need me later, to testify at the trial, of course."

But I just couldn't leave well enough alone. "You always had your heads together. Much closer than one might expect for mere colleagues."

Again that look of perplexed annoyance. "Anna is more than a colleague."

My heart sank. Just as I thought.

"She's the daughter of an old friend, a police buddy. In fact, she's my godchild. Naturally I'm fond of her."

I refused to be mollified. "You seemed to be in a frightful hurry to shut me up when I tried to tell you my theory about Charles Bragg that first afternoon."

"I could see you were getting upset by Anna's questions. I thought they were unfair. But it would have been unprofessional to say so in front of you."

"I never thought of that," I admitted. "But then later you seemed so anxious to pack me off back to Surf City."

He ran his hand through his hair. "I was trying to keep you alive. I did think your accusations sounded credible. That's why after you got thrown from the horse I tried to get you to go home before anything else happened. I was just trying to take care of you."

"I'm quite capable of taking care of myself," I said, somewhat abashed.

"So I noticed. That's why the next thing we know, you're being abducted by a double murderer." He stopped on the bridge to watch the mallards that were now feeding along the stream bank. "There's something else I was going to ask."

"Is this about the letter I took from Scottie's place? If so, I don't see any point in going into it now, unless you're planning to charge me with something."

He smiled. "No." He seemed to consider his next words, and then change his mind. "Did you get to see the wild horses?"

"Not up close." I paused. "But I did see them from a distance. And maybe that's enough. Just to know they're there."

"That's so typical of you," he said.

"What do you mean?" I asked. Was he going to tease me again about my love of nature?

"That you're content just to know that things exist. You don't have to photograph, catalog, identify every bit of flora and fauna you come across. You enjoy just knowing they're there."

He really was rather charming, I thought with a sudden flash of honesty. I regretted that I had burned my bridges as far as he was concerned.

But he wasn't finished. "What I meant to say is..." He hesitated. "I wanted to apologise about the booby incident. You're right. Just to know it's there should be enough. The sighting itself was a rare opportunity, and I should have been satisfied with that."

"Oh," I said, taken aback. "I was going to apologise about that, too. But I got the call to come up here and, well, things just kept happening."

He put his arm around me. "Delilah, let's stop this sparring. You know how I feel about you."

I pulled away and asked, "I do? How, exactly?"

"You must know I want to marry you."

I was stunned. I played for time, saying something about needing to get back to Watson. But he still held my arm, waiting for an answer.

At that moment Watson caught sight of us from the car and gave a loud bark. My reply to Mallory was lost in the startled quacking of a flush of mallards rising from the stream.

Peanut Butter Oatmeal Dog Biscuits

(Watson's favourite)

4 cups whole wheat flour
2 cups oatmeal
½ to ¾ cup peanut butter
2½ cups hot water

Preheat oven to 350°.

Mix all ingredients together, adding more hot water if dough is too stiff. Roll out dough on floured board to ¼ inch thick. Cut with a bone-shaped cookie cutter. Place 1 inch apart on greased cookie sheets.

Bake at 350° until brown and crisp (about 30 minutes).

Makes approx. 6 dozen. Recipe can be halved.

NOTE: Biscuits should be refrigerated or frozen for long-term storage.

Recipe by permission from *Cooking with Calhoune*,
published by Basset Rescue of Southern California

About the Author

Born and raised in Surrey, England, Patricia Guiver began her professional writing career in London's Fleet Street. She now makes her home in Southern California, the setting of her Pet Detective series. There her menagerie includes two cats (Mrs. Tea and Natasha), a cockatiel (Jingle), and a tiny Yorkshire terrier named Paddington. Guiver also writes "The Creature Connection," a pet column for a newspaper group, and in her spare time volunteers for the local Society for the Prevention of Cruelty to Animals. She may be e-mailed at pat4paws@yahoo.com.

MORE MYSTERIES
FROM PERSEVERANCE PRESS
For the New Golden Age

Available now—

***Silence Is Golden,* A Connor Westphal Mystery**
by Penny Warner
ISBN 1-880284-66-9
When the folks of Flat Skunk rediscover gold in them thar hills, the modern-day stampede brings money-hungry miners to the Gold Country town, and headlines for deaf reporter Connor Westphal's newspaper—not to mention murder.

***Death, Bones, and Stately Homes,* A Tori Miracle Pennsylvania Dutch Mystery**
by Valerie S. Malmont
ISBN 1-880284-65-0
Finding a tuxedo-clad skeleton, Tori Miracle fears it could halt Lickin Creek's annual house tour. While dealing with disappearing and reappearing bodies, a stalker, and an escaped convict, Tori unravels the secrets of the Bride's House and Morgan Manor, which the townsfolk wish to hide.

***Slippery Slopes and Other Deadly Things,* A Carrie Carlin Biofeedback Mystery**
by Nancy Tesler
ISBN 1-880284-64-2
Biofeedback practitioner/single mom/amateur sleuth Carrie Carlin is up to her neck in snow, sex, and strangulation when her stress management convention is interrupted by murder on the slopes of a Vermont ski resort.

REFERENCE/MYSTERY WRITING
***How To Write Killer Fiction:* The Funhouse of Mystery & the Roller Coaster of Suspense**
by Carolyn Wheat
ISBN 1-880284-62-6
The highly regarded author of the Cass Jameson legal mysteries explains the difference between mysteries (the art of the whodunit) and novels of suspense (the hero's journey) and offers tips and inspiration for writing in either genre. Wheat shows how to make your book work, from the first word to the final revision.

***Another Fine Mess,* A Bridget Montrose Mystery**
by Lora Roberts
ISBN 1-880284-54-5
Bridget Montrose wrote a surprise bestseller, but now her publisher wants another one. A writers' retreat seems the perfect opportunity to work in the rarefied company of other authors…except that one of them has a different ending in mind.

***Flash Point,* A Susan Kim Delancey Mystery**
by Nancy Baker Jacobs
ISBN 1-880284-56-1
A serial arsonist is killing young mothers in the Bay Area. Now Susan Kim Delancey, California's newly appointed chief arson investigator, is in a race against time to catch the murderer and find the dead women's missing babies—before more lives end in flames.

***Open Season on Lawyers*, A Novel of Suspense**
by Taffy Cannon ISBN 1-880284-51-0

***Too Dead To Swing*, A Katy Green Mystery**
by Hal Glatzer ISBN 1-880284-53-7

***The Tumbleweed Murders*, A Claire Sharples Botanical Mystery**
by Rebecca Rothenberg, completed by Taffy Cannon ISBN 1-880284-43-x

***Keepers*, A Port Silva Mystery**
by Janet LaPierre ISBN 1-880284-44-8
Shamus Award nominee, *Best Paperback Original 2001*

***Blind Side*, A Connor Westphal Mystery**
by Penny Warner ISBN 1-880284-42-1

***The Kidnapping of Rosie Dawn*, A Joe Barley Mystery**
by Eric Wright ISBN 1-880284-40-5
Barry Award, *Best Paperback Original 2000*. Edgar, Ellis, and Anthony Award nominee

***Guns and Roses*, An Irish Eyes Travel Mystery**
by Taffy Cannon ISBN 1-880284-34-0
Agatha and Macavity Award nominee, *Best Novel 2000*

***Royal Flush*, A Jake Samson & Rosie Vicente Mystery**
by Shelley Singer ISBN 1-880284-33-2

***Baby Mine*, A Port Silva Mystery**
by Janet LaPierre ISBN 1-880284-32-4

Forthcoming—

***A Fugue in Hell's Kitchen*, A Katy Green Mystery**
by Hal Glatzer
In New York City in 1939, musician Katy Green's hunt for a stolen music manuscript turns into a fugue of mayhem, madness, and death. Prequel to *Too Dead To Swing.*

***The Affair of the Incognito Tenant*, A Mystery with Sherlock Holmes**
by Lora Roberts
In 1903 in a Sussex village, a young, widowed housekeeper welcomes the mysterious Mr. Sigerson to the manor house in her charge—and unknowingly opens the door to theft, bloody terror, and murder.

Available from your local bookstore or from
Perseverance Press/John Daniel & Co. at (800) 662-8351
or www.danielpublishing.com/perseverance.